J. L. Porro - Believe

Published by **Save The World Productions LLC**
1905 Pico Blvd
Santa Monica, CA 90405-1627

ISBN 979-8-9946890-0-4

For information, contact:
jlstillbelieves@gmail.com

Believe

J. L. PORRO

FROM HOMELESS TO HOLLYWOOD

Dedication

For my father, J.M., who carried me to the land of endless possibility, where the American dream rested gently in the palm of my hand. Your courage became the bridge to my destiny.

For my high school Drama teacher, Ms. Norma Davids, who saw the light within me long before I learned to see it myself. Your faith became the spark that awakened my purpose.

And for my grandmother, Tete, who looked upon a little boy and saw something extraordinary. Your love whispered to my spirit that I was meant for more.

CONTENTS

PROLOGUE

Camagüey, Cuba, July 22, 1990.

Josi Piriz entered the world quietly, as if he already understood the nature of the island that received him. Cuba, at the dawn of the nineties, was a place of measured breath and rationed hope. Scarcity ruled daily life, and oppression lingered in the air like humidity—unseen, unavoidable, clinging to the skin. His mother, Teresa Piriz, cradled him in a modest hospital room while the weight of absence pressed heavily on her chest. His father, Manuel Piriz, was not there.

Manuel was serving the remainder of a thirty-year prison sentence imposed by a government that demanded obedience above all else. Thirteen years of his life had already been claimed by concrete walls and watchful eyes. Josi had been conceived during a conjugal visit—brief, supervised moments of intimacy granted like favors rather than rights. For Teresa, Josi was both miracle and sacrifice. For Manuel, he was proof that something living and unbroken could still emerge from captivity.

Josi was barely two years old when the prison gates finally opened for Manuel—not to freedom, but to exile. Cuba released him the way it released many others: by pushing him away. With little more than a directive and a warning never to return,

Manuel was sent off the island. He took his son with him, believing that whatever pain separation would cause now would be less than the slow suffocation Josi would endure if he stayed.

For decades, Cubans had fled to the United States by any means necessary—on boats, on rafts made of Styrofoam and scrap wood, risking storms, hunger, and the open jaws of the sea. Manuel's escape spared Josi that peril, but not its cost. Teresa stood on the island she loved and hated in equal measure, watching her child disappear into the promise of elsewhere. The suffering was the kind only a mother could fathom: the choice to let go in order to save.

In America, survival took on a different shape. Manuel remarried quickly, believing that stability required a household with two adults, believing that love—any love—was better than none. But the woman he brought into Josi's life carried her own bruises, and she passed them on with open hands. The blows came in silence, behind closed doors, delivered as discipline, justified as necessity. Josi learned early that affection could turn violent without warning, and that chaos was not an interruption of life—it was its rhythm.

They say the earliest years are the most formative. If that is true, then Josi's foundations were poured in fear and confusion. Yet even in those years, there were moments of refuge. Manuel, when he could, took Josi to the movies—dark theaters where the world fell silent and stories flickered larger than life across the screen. Father and son shared popcorn, whispered reactions, and a rare sense of safety. Those afternoons planted something enduring in Josi: a passion for film, for stories that could transport you out of your circumstances. Long before he understood exile or loss, Josi dreamed of becoming a Hollywood filmmaker one day, believing that if stories could save him for two hours at a time, maybe they could save him for good. He grew into a boy alert to shifts in tone, to footsteps in hallways, to the subtle signs that peace was about to shatter. Order never felt natural to him. Disorder did. It was predictable in its own way.

By the time Josi reached adulthood, chaos had become not only familiar but profitable.

In his twenties, Josi discovered a crooked form of success. He worked as a bellboy at The Sumay, a five-star hotel polished to a mirror shine and reserved for the elite—guests who measured their worth in square footage, champagne labels, and discretion. Josi excelled at discretion. He pushed luggage carts, fetched food at impossible hours, and fulfilled requests that never made it into the official ledger. Alongside room keys and welcome smiles, he provided attractive companions and discreet mood enhancers for those willing to pay.

By then, Teresa had made her own way to the United States. Manuel, worn down by years of labor and unresolved battles, had passed away. Josi was alone in the most crowded of cities, untethered from the past yet shaped entirely by it. His father had been a welder—a man who worked with fire and metal—but he had never wanted that life for his son. Manuel believed Josi was meant to elevate the family's standing, to become more than a laborer. Ironically, in trying to spare his son the hardships of his own trade, Manuel had left him without one.

Josi was not following in anyone's footsteps. He was veering deliberately off the beaten path.

At The Sumay, he found an audience that rewarded him generously. His clients showed their appreciation in ways far exceeding a bellboy's wages: sports cars, champagne-soaked nights, jewelry that caught the light just right, designer clothes, and vacations that blurred continents together. It was a life parallel to that of the elite he served—close enough to touch, but never fully claimed. Still, it was intoxicating.

Daniela certainly thought so.

She was demanding, sharp, and born into money. Daniela moved through the world with the ease of someone who had never questioned whether she belonged. Being with her stirred something restless in Josi—a need to prove himself worthy of her world by any means necessary. He felt the pressure acutely. Without a trade, without a pedigree, and without patience for conventional ladders, Josi relied on the only currency he had learned to trust: access.

Not everyone at The Sumay was impressed.

Mr. Durant, the hotel manager, watched Josi with thinly veiled contempt. Rules mattered to Durant. So did appearances. Josi bent both. Their days unfolded like a game of cat and mouse—except Durant was not playing. He was hunting. All he needed was one undeniable reason to justify Josi's dismissal. Josi, for his part, kept the patrons happy, and in a place like The Sumay, that counted for something. Sometimes, it counted for everything.

Outside the hotel, Josi's life was stitched together by loyalty. Benjamin, perpetually broke and driving a clunker, borrowed Josi's sports car without ceremony, raided his closet, and slept on his plush sofa bed like it was his own. Melchi, a successful real estate investor, didn't need handouts, but he received Josi's generosity all the same. They were brothers in everything but blood.

And then there was Julio.

Julio, Josi's stepfather, was the quiet engine behind Josi's yearning for something more tangible—something real. Raised in Cuba, Julio was a man forged by necessity, a jack of all trades who believed a man's worth was measured by what he could build, fix, or endure. He never missed an opportunity to remind Josi of this. Every comparison was a verdict. Every comment sharpened the ache Josi carried: the sense that love had to be earned, proven, justified.

Julio had no interest in Josi's explanations, his hustle, or his half-glimpses of success. To Julio, shortcuts were failures in disguise.

And Josi, standing between the life he had and the life he wanted, could feel the distance widening—one choice, one secret, one inevitable reckoning at a time.

BELIEVE

ACT ONE

As I stood in front of my father Manuel Piriz's tombstone, staring at the passage engraved on his headstone—*For we walk by FAITH, not by sight*—it felt as if I were reading his last words of advice. It had been a hot summer night in July of 1992, approaching my third birthday. I was in bed in my mother's house in the beautiful Cuban province of Camaguey. My father was exiled to Spain after serving almost fourteen years in one of the worst prisons in Cuba and had no intention of leaving me behind. He was an outstanding leader in his community, an entrepreneur, a devout Catholic, and a kind and charitable man. Everything had been seized—his businesses, assets, and money—and yet he considered himself one of the lucky ones. Most of the men with whom he allied against the Castro regime faced a firing squad. Communist Cuba was not the place where my father wanted me to grow up. My stoic grandmother, her hair up in rollers, watched as my father, with his slicked-back hair and restless soul—picked me up from my bed and carried me out the front door, a suitcase in his other hand. My mother, a dressmaker and housewife in her twenties with waist-length hair, ran to the door, crying hysterically. My grandmother restrained her. My mother was aware of the arrangement, now in action, but nothing could prepare her for the separation anxiety triggered by that fateful moment. My father had convinced her of what was best for me. It was a golden opportunity to live free and be spared from the atrocities of communism. Outside, my father handed the suitcase to a cab driver as my mother desperately tried to disentangle herself, looking on hopelessly, as the taxi pulled away. The year was 1998—I was living with my father in Little Havana, a neighborhood in Miami, Florida. I was eight years old. Shy, with one-length hair and nearly as black as my father's. He looked the same, except he no longer sported his *Happy Days*-do. The sound of crickets partially filled the theater as moviegoers sat scattered about, watching *E.T.* I sat Indian style in my seat, popcorn bag in lap, munching away. Orchestra music softly played.

"Stay," said Elliot. My father extended his forearm, which was covered with thick, black hair, and handed me a cup of Coke. Eyes glistening and lashes soaked, I leaned into the straw. After the movie, I remember him saying to me,

"Why do you cry so much?" And I had no idea why. In hindsight, that seemingly insignificant moment would illuminate my purpose in life. I believe God made me emotional for a reason, and the magic of filmmaking was that very reason. It was clear that my dad was hardened by more than a dozen years in prison not to mention losing everything he had worked so hard for, so he wanted me, his only son, to grow up to be macho. Later, I realized that the films he was watching may have played a role in my upbringing. He was a big fan of John Wayne and eventually Clint Eastwood, Charles Bronson, and Chuck Norris. Fast forward two years: I was ten, and my father had married a woman, who won him over by showering me with toys and affection. It had been just the two of us until she came along. And by that point, eight years had gone by since I had been separated from my mom. I resented having no memory of her, mainly because I witnessed the love and care my buddies received from their moms. My father gave me all he could, but there was an indelible void in my upbringing since my mother couldn't leave the communist island. My father had set the wheels in motion to bring her to the States, but it was going to take some time. Outside our modest apartment building, boys dressed in rags and played stickball in the street, while upstairs in my room, I watched *Aladdin* on my television, and toys were spread out on the floor.From my doorway, I watched my father comb his hair in the bathroom mirror. And so, I wanted to emulate him. Therefore, I began my search for grooming supplies. I walked to a nightstand, opened a drawer, and found it empty. After looking around the bedroom, I took my search to the bathroom, where I carefully placed a step stool against the sink and climbed on it. I pulled open a drawer containing hair products and a hairbrush, so I styled my hair as best as a boy could. My new stepmother yelled at me in her Cuban accent.

"You think you're some kind of movie star?" She paused for a second as if to figure out what she was going to say next to further tear me down.

"Stop looking in the mirror. Only girls look in the mirror. Look at this mess." She reared on me in her stupid bandana ready to terrorize me. She struck me repeatedly on the head, face, and shoulders. One blow caught my ear, which left me hearing a whooshing sound.

"I'm sick and tired of it," she yelled, leaving me cringing in one corner of the bathroom.

"I'm not your slave!" A knock sounded at the door.

"Can Josi come out and play?" a boy asked.

"No. Josi has to clean up his room." The boys' voices faded in the distance, followed by a door slamming. I stared at the ceiling, crying. Some years later, my father had an accident at a construction site where he worked as a welding contractor. He hadn't been scheduled to work that day. It was his birthday, and we had planned to go to a baseball game. But the construction crew was ahead of schedule, and my father was the only one with the necessary experience to do the job. And he knew what his work meant for our lives, so he never missed a day, scheduled or otherwise. As fate would have it, a poorly secured pile of rebar tumbled down on him. He was rushed to the hospital, where he died of internal hemorrhaging. Again, I found myself yelling, "Why?" "Why?" Not long after the memorial service, my mother arrived at a nearby city where I went to live with her and her new husband. I felt like a stranger there. Her husband resented my presence. He asked me when I was planning on moving out. I was still in high school and working part-time, but I knew I couldn't take the insults any longer. I lied to my mom and said that I was moving in with a friend. My new home address was anywhere from a park, a beach, or a parking garage. I even slept in an out-of-order water fountain, which blocked the cool breeze in winter, but when it rained it had me running for cover. There wasn't any time for self-pity. I just knew that my father hadn't given me the gift of opportunity to just die on the street. He wanted me to *walk by faith and not by sight*. So, I got myself a tent and found a place on the beach and off the beaten path where the cops wouldn't harass me or drive me home and where psychological terrorism would resume. I always looked at the bright side of life, because I knew God had a plan for me. And knowing that this too shall pass, it was all the mustard seed of faith that I needed to keep moving forward. Anger sparked the fire inside me and fear itself made me braver through my trials and tribulations. Years later… It was 2013, and I was finally off the street. Now with a GED, I was able to get a full-time job at the hotel where I'd been a part-timer, I had taken up residence at a condo in Key Biscayne, Miami Florida. The island life there was distinctive and sophisticated. It wasn't unusual to see someone driving a golf cart loaded with groceries. My guilty pleasure was cheeseburgers, but sometimes I'd cross the street to Carmine's for some pizza. Carmine's wasn't just food, it was a religious experience. I could take a bike ride to the lighthouse and catch a sunset, stroll to the beach, or have tropical drinks with friends overlooking the ocean. It was paradise. Yeah, I lived in luxury. I had a beautiful, whip-smart girlfriend, who I'd convinced that I made my money in the stock market. But I was the party favors supplier and companions' liaison for the hottest hotel on the beach. Why was I questioning the choices I've made? My lifestyle? Did I even have a choice? It was 9:36 pm I was twenty-three, with revealing, sad eyes. I didn't feel burdened with responsibility, the way a president, general, or scientist does, but just in the way that anyone with a little humanity might. It felt as if I was stuck in a place where the fork in my road had led me. The escorts that I offered as paid companions to my clients were escorts long before I came around and weren't pressured into it. They were also brought to their crossroads. And my father believed a man without a dream dies, so was I dying inside? I never fathomed myself of doing such things. So, I lay asleep hugging a journal, wrapped in my comforter with one leg out on my oversized bed, burdened by my sins. *Citizen Kane* played on my massive flat screen, with the volume turned down. My appreciation for the classics had been passed down by my father, of course, since we shared an affinity for the cinema. On my nightstand stood a framed picture of my dad on his knees next to me, a small boy at the time, hugging my dad while smiling at the camera. Next to it was a reference book for screenwriting, which had a typewriter on the cover and a bookmark sticking out of it, pointing at me like a condemning finger, reminding me to finish what I'd started. The phone rang, waking me up. I felt around my bed, grabbed it, and saw who was calling as well as who was startled by my phone. It was my boisterous friend Melchi who sounds exactly like *Tony Montana. We* met in high school when he didn't speak a lick of English. He never took anything seriously—yet, surprisingly, he did well for himself in the real estate game. Melchi jumped off the couch and yelled,

"Holy shit, I'm going to be late." Ran into my bedroom and hugged me as I was speaking.

"David ... No, I was just watching TV... No problem." I hung up with David, a resident at the hotel where I worked.

"Have a great trip, my brother," I said to Melchi.

"Thank you, my brother. Call me when you come out," he said.

"Come out where?"

"The closet." He laughed his ass out the door and I just shook my head. Then I made a call to my friend Benjamin.

"Benji, I need my car ... With the cell phone wedged against my shoulder, I got dressed. "Yes, I need it yesterday ... and by the way, you said your furniture's mid-century ... yeah well, my chiropractor would say it's medieval ... don't worry about it. I'll pay for the movers next time you need help with your torture devices." I pocketed my phone. Benjamin, my fun-loving and object-oriented friend in his thirties, swapped back car keys with me. Benjamin wasn't a bad guy, he just felt he had something to prove. We both came from humble beginnings.

"You think I can borrow it again on Saturday?" he asked.

"Next weekend, it's all yours." I headed to my car.

"I'm taking Daniela away this weekend, and don't mention it—it's a surprise."

"Who am I gonna tell?"

"You owe me a shirt from your aunt's boutique." Benji shrugged.

"Sure, when she leaves it to me."

"Hey, since you're going out of town, can I use the apartment?"

"I left a key for you at the front desk." Benjamin looked over at me.

"What...?"

"What...? If only I listened to my messages," I said mocking him. Then he struggled with the reluctant door of his faded red-turned-pink clunker. I understood why Benji liked my matte-black Audi R8. It was a head-turner. I opened my sunglasses holder to find it empty, and I shook my head. Benjamin checked his hair in the rear-view mirror, pulled a pair of sunglasses off his head, and pulled around the parking lot. He doesn't steal from me, he just never asks for permission to use my things, which he knows that I would never say no to, so I'm just sparing myself from futile dialogue with Benji. His car lurched forward, backfired, and left a cloud of smoke. He came from a well-to-do family, but he blew his money away partying. I don't have people with deep pockets to bail me out, and all I asked for was little consideration from time to time.

"Love you," Benjamin yelled out the window. At the sight of my gas gauge on empty, I let out a sigh, lowered my window, and yelled back,

"I love you too." Then I thought to myself, *I deserve an entire wardrobe*." I raised my window and drove away. Next, I pulled into the nearest gas station on the island, and I left the pump filling up my car while I walked in the market for some much-needed high-octane for myself. I reached into the cooler for a Red Bull and overheard a little boy speaking to his mother.

"But I want cookies."

"No," said his mom, shaking her head as I got in line behind them.

"You have plenty."

"But these are the Chewy Gooey ones." She shook her head while she was handing money to the cashier.

"Fine," he said. Then he dropped his gaze and took a step toward the aisle. I snagged the bag of cookies out of his hand. I could feel him staring at me as I paid the cashier. The mom and boy exited the market. After an exchange of pleasantries with the cashier, I followed them out to their car. I extended my arm to hand him the cookies while holding the mom's gaze, seeking her approval. She pursed her lips, shook her head, and said to the boy,

"Nathaniel, you're something else." I handed him the cookies.

"What do you say?"

"Thank you," the boy said.

"It's my pleasure." The mom smirked while she shook her head at me.

"Come on, Mom—they're Chewy Gooey."She mouthed the words,

As I drove above on the highway, the city was framed by the Miami skyline, which could only be described as a bright, lively, colorful postcard that read *Welcome to the Magic City*. Home to the musical genius of Emilio and Gloria Estefan, (Film Star) Andy Garcia, Carlos Alfonso's painting and sculpture along the streets of Ocean Drive, the museum of Celia (The Queen of Salsa). On a personal level, Miami is also the home and very special place where my late father wished for me to grow up, spared of the atrocities of communism. And where I would learn what it means to have a dream because he would've wanted me to have the freedom to chase it. At a fast-food joint, a drive-thru attendant took money from me. Art Deco buildings brightened Ocean Drive in neon colors, palm trees swayed, and waves greeted the sandcastles as I cruised the boulevard. I pulled over by a park and honked. After recognizing my car, a homeless woman in dreads named Sherri gave me a cheered-up smile, and I handed her a fast-food bag and soda. She opened the bag and blew a kiss to the sky, then bit into her burger. *Coming from a communist country and having an ex-political prisoner as a father, I was educated on how food is abundant for us in the States, but not so for others in countries such as Cuba and many others throughout the world, so the highest honor to God as I knew it to be, was to break bread with those to whom food was not abundant.* The car radio told me it was 10:38 pm. A typical night on Miami Beach, with its lofty palm trees dancing with the breeze, models, and exotic cars. I arrived at the valet stand of the Sumay Hotel, where I worked. At the same moment, Daniela, a dauntless girl in her twenties with a tight body and a bob haircut, approached me with a clipboard in hand, leaving the velvet rope line full of models behind.

"I'm sorry, sir, but you can't park here," she said.

"Do you know who I am?" I responded as I posed up. Daniela scowled and got in my face.

"No. Why don't you refresh my memory?" So, I grabbed her by the back of her head and made out with her. Daniela was my girlfriend. She laughed. I rushed off. A female voice in the crowd called out,

"Daniela." Daniela turned to see who it was.

"I'll be right there," she said. Then yelled out to me,

"Drinks later?" I turned, walking backward.

"Mia's? Around twelve?" Daniela nodded and blew me a kiss. I caught the imaginary kiss and pocketed it in my jeans, then turned the other way, heading for the delivery entrance. Looking around hesitantly, I approached a side entrance of the hotel and typed in a code on the door. As I walked onto the charcoal tile floor inside the intriguing hotel, with black iron Indonesian sculptures and dark wood wall treatments throughout, peaceful meditation-like music played. The hotel had played host to famous actors, world-renowned musicians, and royalty. I pressed the button for the elevator. Its doors opened, and I rushed inside and pushed the button for the thirty-eighth floor. After the doors closed, I let out a sigh of relief, because employees of the hotel were strictly prohibited from visiting residents and guest floors outside of our scheduled working hours. As I approached David's suite, I heard thumping bass playing inside. I knocked on the door. David, a tall, athletic, successful Brazilian entrepreneur, with enough confidence for a band geek to hit on the most popular girl in school, greeted me.

"Josi, good to see you. Come on in." David led me inside with a smile that must've had something to do with the panoramic views of Miami's skyline from up there. I was beginning to crack a smile myself. The music blared from the living room, where the scene was young and sexy. After David talked into a man's ear for a moment, he turned to me. I handed him an envelope, and he gave me the "secret money handshake" before leading me down a hallway, away from the crowd. We walked inside his bedroom where two curvaceous Brazilian girls—Vani, David's wife, and her friend Jezebel—were spread out on the bed, naked. David's smile wasn't just about the panorama. He poured me a drink. *Let me just say this, I never claimed to be perfect, but I always believed that love was earned. And though I couldn't help but see the menu there, I had no intention of ordering.*

"Hey, Josi," Vani said and waved me over.

"Hi." I took a step closer to the naked girls in bed.

"Jezebel is visiting from Sao Paolo," Vani said. I waved.

"Josi, come sit," Vani said as she patted the bed.

"There's plenty of room," Jezebel chimed in.

"I have to go."

"Awe," Jezebel continued.

"My girlfriend's waiting."

"Que pena," Jezebel said. David handed me a drink, which I drained.

"Next time, bring her," he said. I grinned incredulously as I shook David's hand.

"Thanks for the drink," I said as I made for the door. I took the elevator down to the hotel lobby and headed for the side door when a Chinese girl in hotel uniform saw me and hollered,

"Hi, Josi."

"Shhh." Later that night at Mia's, a polished yet unassuming Italian restaurant adorned with oversized leather booths and retro table lamps, I met up with Daniela. We sat away from the crowd. Daniela scrutinized a message on her phone while I talked. A waiter poured us champagne. We toasted.

"To medical school," I said.

"It was just an interview."

"Daniela, if I had the grades to just interview for something as prestigious as medical school, I'd throw myself a parade. And didn't you say your interview went well?" Daniela nods and gives me a smirk.

"So, I've been reading this book, and ever since, I've been curious about existential questions.

Daniela looked up at me and dropped her head back in her lap, where there was a seemingly better conversation going on over her cell phone.

"Listening," she said.

"What if we're missing the big picture? Are we living our best life? Or are we just content with the status quo?"

"Hey," I said. Daniela looked up at me.

"I'm listening."

"Remember, it's you who insisted I get a library card—to read more—to have more to say."

"And I created a monster," Daniela said, staring at her lap. Then looked up at me and feigned a laugh.

"Just kidding. You have ketchup on your face."

I took my napkin and wiped my mouth. And ... With her head still buried in her lap, Daniela responded,

"I am all ears."

"I feel that I have important things to say, but it feels like no one is ever listening?"

"I listen," Daniela said. I shifted in my seat.

"Okay," I went on.

"I feel like everything and everyone in the universe is connected, like in the movie *Phenomenon* with John Travolta." Daniela put her phone away.

"Don't tell me you're reading a Scientology book."

"No. What I'm getting at is the disconnect we all have from one another, and it's snowballing. It's as if—" Daniela's phone sounded a message alert, and she pulled it out of her purse and typed away.

"Exactly," I said.

"I'm sorry—it was Dinah. She's having Ethan problems." Our waiter brought our dessert. Daniela ate as I stared at her vacantly.

"What?" Daniela showed me her entire grill.

"I have something in my teeth?"

"Yes, you have a little piece of text between your teeth."

"Dork." She smiled sarcastically, dug into her dessert, and said,

"This is amazing." I smirked and sipped champagne in defeat, not celebration. Back at my condo, we walked inside to find Benjamin on my made-up sofa bed. He must've had another fight with Becca, his girlfriend. It was constant. Daniela removed her heels, and I followed her into the bedroom. The next morning, Daniela kissed me on my forehead. My head was buried in my pillow, with one eye open, but when I raised my head to say goodbye, the sound of the front door closing assured me I was too late. What could I say? I wasn't a morning person. I did my best work in the evening. Benjamin was still passed out on the sleeper—I knew this because I could hear him snoring. And it didn't help that Daniela left the door open. But I never complained as I was secretly longing for a family of my own. The disconnect in my family and my toxic upbringing played major roles in how I viewed family and what and whom I allowed in my life. Anyhow, I broke off half a zany and grabbed a breakfast beer out of the fridge to wash it down. I poured the beer in my Thermos bottle for my ritual walk on the sand. The sun cut through the clouds, and I started to get that panicky, racy feeling, brought on by my anxiety intensified by a massive hangover—wait a minute—aah... *Maybe our intuition is trying to tell us something, like Are we off course in the whole scheme of our dutiful existence? Or are we not taking proper care of ourselves? Or both.* Well, the zany had officially taken effect, and I could finally breathe it all in, the cotton candy clouds providing shade, the exhilarating breeze, and the gentle break of the waves rendering the most soothing familiar sound. I sat back on the sand, just appreciating the view. When I got upstairs, I heard the shower running and noticed Benjamin had sloppily made up the still-pulled-out sofa bed, which meant he'd be my guest a little while longer. What are friends for, anyway, right? I walked into my bedroom, shut the door behind me, and wrote in my journal. I waved goodbye to Benjamin as he casually walked off, wearing one of my never-worn tag-still-on shirts. Benjamin had become very resourceful with my resources. My cell phone played jazz, alerting me of the time, so I got dressed and headed out the door. Later, at the hotel, now in my bellboy uniform, I placed a suitcase on a luggage stand in a guest's bedroom and followed the guest to the living room. He was Mr. Belyakov, a towering Russian man in his forties, a regular at the Sumay. He stopped near the entrance as if he had just realized something.

"Will there be anything else, Mr. Belyakov?" I asked. He leaned toward me. "Can you get us some girls for tonight?" Then he signaled toward a man seated on the couch. I pulled out my cell phone and swiped through some images of the kind of companions the Russians meant.

"Will these do?" I asked confidently knowing that I had the most alluring women in town. He smiled and nodded. Mr. Belyakov did a line of coke on the coffee table in his suite, then gestured to me, and I did a line. Then Mr. Belyakov walked over to the man on the couch and showed him the selection of girls from my phone. And I didn't understand what they were saying in Russian, but I knew what an ear-to-ear smile meant—another fat tip from another satisfied customer. Later, I gulped a frozen cocktail at the pool bar. "AHHHH! Brain freeze." And I shot a thumbs-up at the bartender. Then, outside the hotel, Mick, a showbiz-connected man, got in the back of a town car and extended his hand out the window with a business card. I took it.

"Call me if you ever get that script written. The story's got some potential. I'll see what I can do. But remember, you only get one shot with Hollywood. Don't blow it with an amateur script. You must polish it into twenty-four karat gold." I acknowledged the business card.

"Thanks, Mick." The tinted window rose as the town car drove off and it was back to business. The girls already gave me a cut, and this was the perk of being the middleman. No one knew you were double-dipping, and nobody cared. My procurement service wasn't regulated or tax-deductible, nor was it in my job description, and I operated with discretion. One might've said that I had a broader understanding of hospitality. Later, a man's voice with a French accent called out,

"Where is Josi?" A Mexican bellboy pushing a luggage cart up the hotel driveway responded.

“He’s flagging down a taxi for a hotel guest, sir.” Mr. Durant, the hotel manager with freakish white veneers, paced the driveway. Durant, as we call him, was not a team player. He walked inside the hotel, allowing the door to close on the Mexican bellboy’s overloaded luggage cart.

“*Que pendejo este tipo*,” said the Mexican bellboy. The shade surrounding the Sumay, one of the tallest buildings on the beach, was an unspoken perk that I greatly appreciated. And the square footage of my office was immeasurable because I wasn’t confined to a desk. And my salary wasn’t contingent on a performance evaluation—I made certain of that. The downside to my operation was the risk of getting caught. If I did, I would have lost it all—there was no Plan B. And what I meant by “lose it all,” I mean everything—, the easy money, the sports car, the luxury condo, and everything else that comes with the good life, including the girl. Daniela was not the type of girl who’d be satisfied with tuna out of a can, even if it was albacore. But I wasn’t the slightest bit worried. Everybody loved me at the Sumay. What was there to worry about, except making enough money to satisfy Daniela’s whims? I had this—or was it just the opposite? Was I subconsciously hoping to get caught? I cunningly reached inside a taxi’s passenger window, placed some merchandise in my pocket, and walked off. There was no way I’d risk my locker being searched or stolen. Merchandise was costly, so I partnered up with some associates who happened to be hidden in plain sight. Okay, so I was no saint, but I also didn’t have an inheritance. So, a tow truck driver handed me a bag, and I shoved it in my pocket. A single *WOOP* came from a police vehicle driving behind the tow truck, and I shrewdly pointed in the distance as if I were giving him directions. And then I walked away composed, but on edge. The thrill of the score was suddenly creeping in on my nerves, and, as alluring as becoming a Hollywood writer was to me, there was no guarantee that I would end up a working writer. At the very least, I could always count on a paycheck at The Sumay. Night fell as a pair of high-class hookers, a blonde hooker called Gigi, and Nin, an Asian hooker, strolled out of the hotel. As Nin continued, Gigi stopped to check her cell phone. Lurking in the shadows around the side of the hotel, I pocketed my cell phone and collected money from Nin. Then Gigi handed me money as we crossed paths. After work, the hotel staff gathered at the Joint, a bar we frequented. Everyone was enjoying drinks at the end of the night, compliments from Mr. Macbridan, the owner of the Sumay. Mr. Macbridan was a Scotsman in his fifties. A man of few words but a permanent smile. Most of the guys, my immediate coworkers, were in jeans and T-shirts, like me. The managers were in their business attire, as they didn't have uniforms to change out of. I stood at one end of the bar, chatting with coworkers, mostly doormen and bellboys. And as one does in high school, we sat in our respective groups, gossiping about others, the day's events, and an occasional scandal witnessed firsthand by a hotel employee. The guys and I were drinking and laughing. Standing next to me was Josh, a rambunctious twenty-something coworker from Jersey.

"Daniela doesn't ask how you can afford luxuries way out of a bellboy's salary?" he asks.

"I might have led her to believe that I made some money in the stock market." Josh shot me a look. Then, Jeremy, in his thirties, our easy-going front office manager, grabbed my shoulder.

"Hey Joe, it's date night with my wife. What movie should we watch?"

"You said your wife's a schoolteacher?"

"She is."

"*Scent Of a Woman.* She'll appreciate the wisdom."

"*Scent Of a Woman,* it is. Thanks, Josi."

"No problem." Jeremy returned to his suited cohorts. Then some cute girls walked past, smiling.

"Girls, this is Josh. He's wanted … by NASA." Josh shook his head.

"No?" I said to Josh. I looked at the girls and then back to Josh.

"You mean to tell me your Ted Bundy stare works better than saying something—anything?" "I know what I'm doing."

"So, how'd ya make out today?" Josh asked.

"I can eat."

"Ya shyster." Mr. Macbridan addressed the staff.

"Do you guys want to know who I want as the next general manager of the Sumay Miami?"

"Yes, who?" replied an employee. All eyes were on Mr. Macbridan as I inattentively sipped my drink at the end of the bar.

"Josi," shouted out Mr. Macbridan. I choked a little and held up a napkin to my nose as some of my whiskey came out of it. The guys congratulated me. I fixed my eyes on Mr. Durant as he walked out of the bar. If there was one way to make Mr. Durant like me any less, this was it—an epic insult to the hotel manager, with all his credentials and experience, getting passed over for the general manager position, by me, a bellboy.

"That's my boy!"

"You da man, Josi!"

"That's what's up!" random voices yelled out. Mr. Mcbridan raised his glass. "To Josi."

"Cheers," everyone toasted. The guys and I clink-clanked our glasses together.

"This is happening," I said, narrowing my eyes and talking with my hands.

"You guys put something in my drink?" My coworkers had a good laugh. Josh hugged me and talked in my ear—something about taking over the world—typical testosterone and alcohol-fueled bar banter. Once the shockwave settled and I could think straight, I realized, *this is a game changer. A once-in-a-lifetime opportunity, because I've never heard of anyone promoted from bellboy to general manager. This must be one of God's miracles. And I haven't even been playing by the rules, so how could this be? Am I deserving of such a miracle? Well, I am kind to others, and—maybe this is God's way of saying—I see you. Maybe good guys do finish first. And maybe being good doesn't necessarily mean being perfect.* Moments later, Mr. Durant returned and walked over to a couple of young girls remaining in the group. He interpreted a smile from one of them as an invitation to lay one on her, so he kissed his unsuspecting victim, which became discernibly upset and ditched the group. The others scurried off after her, and a contentious Durant advanced on Jeremy.

"If he doesn't come in to work tomorrow, he's fired," Mr. Durant warned Jeremy. Mr. Durant pointed our way.

"Don't even think about coming in late tomorrow," said Mr. Durant as he left hastily.

"Who was he talking to?" I asked.

"Who else?" Josh said.

"I don't work tomorrow." Jeremy walked over to me.

"Durant says if you don't show up for work tomorrow, you're fired." I squinted in confusion.

"But I'm off tomorrow?"

"I know," said Jeremy. Jeremy and I looked at one another and laughed.

"Bartender, shots all around," I hollered.

"Let's get some coke," Josh said.

"Yeah," my coworkers shouted.

"Let's get some hookers," yelled one of the guys. The guys clamored and hooted. *I'm relishing a win for the underdog—for all of us. It's why the fellas are so excited, heck, if it can happen for me, it can happen for any of them. The glaring difference between Mr. Durant and myself is that he's way more educated on paper, but I'm keen on the ole' cliché, "You catch more flies with honey". Or something along the lines of what I have in mind. I genuinely believe that kindness trumps arrogance. Intellectual bullies are bullies, nevertheless.* Two days later, crossing the lobby, I ran into Josh.

"Hey Josh."

"Durand asked me where you were, so I told him you were flagging down a taxi for a guest."

"I was."

"Yeah, where? Hotel California?"

"Those lyrics aren't just about cocaine," I said. Josh shot me a look.

"But mostly cocaine," I said.

"We're gonna get twisted this weekend or what?" asked Josh. A fist bump from Josh, and he rolled away a luggage cart. *I probably should've quit taking these risks while I was ahead, but the money was too good to pass up and it was cash in hand. The general manager position didn't take effect until I completed the manager-in-training program, which took a minimum of two years. What if the hotel group sells the hotel during that time? I would've wasted all that time for nothing and lost everything I had. And since accepting the GM position would consist of working one-on-one with a supervisor from every department, I'd have to say Sayonara side hustle. Which reminds me, Durant couldn't possibly be pissed about not getting the GM position at the hotel—he must have options galore—and I can't imagine him accepting to work under me or sticking around the hotel for another two years to witness my coronation.*

"Josi, I need you to pick up some food for Mr. Silva at Saki's," Jeremy said.

He handed me money, and I scurried off. What a concept—getting paid for running errands and fulfilling the whims of others. I couldn't have created a better job for myself, as I had already helped everyone without expecting a thing. Mr. Durand smirked as I crossed the lobby. Then I thought I heard, "Gotcha," from a distance. Was it Durand? Was that addressed to me? Or was I becoming paranoid? I partied out and leaned into the bar at Saki's, a trendy sushi bar and lounge dimly lit by candles, black lights, and an oversized chandelier. The décor was colorful and eclectic. Tatiana, a sassy, tattooed bartender, got the bar ready for service. I placed money on the counter as she approached me.

"Hi, Josi."

"Hey." Tatiana handed me the carry-out.

"Hung over much?" I nodded wearily. Tatiana prepared me a vodka Red Bull, then handed me the *eye-opener*.

"You need Jesus, Josi." I rolled my eyes, drained my vodka Red Bull, and flapped my imaginary wings.

"I'm back." Tatiana shook her head as I walked away with the take-out. Back at the hotel, David placed the takeout on his counter and handed me money.

"Thank you, Josi."

"Enjoy, sir," I said with a wink. As I walked down the hall of David's floor, my cell phone vibrated in my pocket, and I answered it.

"Hello."

"Hey," Daniela said.

"Hey."

"Did you have lunch already?" she asked.

"No, I've been too busy. We're—"

"So we can't have lunch together?" she asked.

"I didn't say that—you don't let me finish. Let me see my list, cause we're almost at a hundred percent—hold on," I said as I reached into my pocket and took out a paper. "If you want to have lunch, it has to be now, cause in about an hour I have nonstop check-ins."

"Too busy for UM School of Medicine's newest addition?"

"Whoa, that's great news."

"Aha. Now how about that lunch?"

"Lucky's Pub in fifteen minutes," I said.

"Okay. Wait, what are you going to have?"

"A burger."

"A burger?" she complained. "Fine…" She withdrew with a sigh. *Daniela wasn't brought up on burgers and fries and I wasn't either, but for different reasons. She ate out with her folks at trendy restaurants, and when I ate out with my dad, our think was Pizza □ la door.*

“Okay, bye,” I said, hanging up.

“Hey, let me get a burger and...” I said, placing our food order over the phone. House music played in my pocket, so I took out my other cell phone.

“Can you hold on one second?” … “Thanks.”

“Hello … Yes, eight o’clock … Right, the blonde one and the Asian one. ... Dale!” I quickly switched back to the other phone.

“Sorry about that. I’ll have—□ Inside Lucky’s, a good old Irish pub, adorned with the green cushions and dark wood that was a burger and beer staple, I grabbed a quiet booth. Around the back was a pool table and dartboard, another more casual gathering place for the employees of the Sumay—not so much for the managers. As usual, the outdoor area was taken by snowbirds. The door opened, and the overwhelming glare of the sunlight’s brightness peeked in. The waitress, a friendly Southern belle, delivered the food to the table as Daniela approached.

“I’ll be right back with your refills.”

“Can I please have some lemon for my soda?” I asked.

“Sure thing, handsome.” Daniela gave me the evil eye. I shook my head.

“Here you go,” the waitress said as she dropped off my lemon wedges.

“Thank you.”

“Is there anything else I can get you folks?” the waitress kindly asked.

"No, thank you," Daniela responded with a fake smile.

"Daniela?" Daniela scowled at me.

"She's in uniform, not a Halloween costume—she's just doing her job."

"I'm sorry, I just hate that girls are always gawking at you."

"And I hate that guys always want to whisk you off to Dubai." This earned a headshake from Daniela. I gave her a look, took an envelope out of my pocket, and slid it over to her. Written on the envelope was *Congrats on UM Med!*

"What's this?" she asked. I shrugged and said,

"Only one way to find out." Daniela ripped open the envelope and took out a leaflet. Inside the envelope was a brochure for Little Palm Island—a luxury resort in the Florida Keys.

"Oh my God, seriously?" She scrutinized the pamphlet.

"Grab your bathing suits," I said.

"Oh my God, you're the best—I'm going shopping."

"Don't you have to go to work?" I asked.

"After I shop for new bikinis. Wait. I just told you I got in."

"I wrote on the envelope before walking over here. I just figured you could use a distraction from the applications and interviews." Daniela gave me a lingering kiss. And just shy of the entrance, she blew me another and bolted. Later, I walked over to see Jeremy. I figured he wanted to talk to me about my big promotion, so I walked into the office excited about becoming the next general manager of the Sumay, my hot girlfriend on her way to being a doctor, and our trip to the Keys. Life was perfect.

"You need me?" I asked.

"Have a seat," Jeremy said. I took a candy out of a candy jar and unwrapped it.

"You're destined for great things, Josi."

I smiled a little as I sucked on the candy.

"Don't let your gifts go to waste."

I shook my head.

"I won't."

"I hope you make the most of this opportunity."

"Definitely."

"Everything in life happens for a reason," Jeremy said.

"I agree."

"You and I both knew it was only a matter of time." I smirked.

"And you underestimated Durant's willingness to expose you."

"What?"

"During Mr. Durant's witch-hunt, some footage of you selling molly was uncovered."

"That was candy," I said.

"Candy, the hooker?"

"But—"

"Josi, you're on camera on the guest floors outside your shift and out of uniform. That alone is cause for termination. You know the rules. Just be grateful Durant didn't have his way with you."

"His way?"

"A sting operation where you go to prison for a very long time."

"Why didn't he?"

"Macbridan." I took this in, and I was suddenly concerned about my future. How, if I was so beloved by my superiors, revered by my coworkers, and appreciated by the guests, had I allowed "running errands" to go so far as to get myself fired? And now I lost most of my clients—hotel guests.

"I'm sorry, Josi." Jeremy handed me a form and pointed to the bottom with a pen. I signed, walked to the door, and turned the knob.

"Josi ... *If you get all tangled up, just tango on.*" I smiled a little and sauntered out into the void I had created for myself. With my eyes starting to well up, I just needed a moment alone to compose myself—so I walked in the bathroom and let my tears run. As I changed out of my uniform for the last time, I knew I had blown it. But I wasn't ready to face it. I needed to be alone. I didn't know how to let the girl that I planned on marrying and starting a family with, that I was a brainless idiot. And not to mention all the lies that she's going to find out when she probes me. The lies about my job and about how I got her to go out with me. As I approached my car, my VIP service cell phone played "Mr. Brightside" again. I looked at the phone and saw it was David calling. I knew if I answered, I was about as ripe as one can be for a downward spiral. And maybe Jeremy was right. Things could've ended much worse for me. I reluctantly dropped the VIP service phone in the trash outside. Maybe it was divine intervention and maybe the only way for me to let go of such a lucrative but risky business, yet I knew I could never walk away from it, otherwise—not at that time. Then I placed my cell phone on silent. I wasn't up to talking to anybody at that moment, especially not Daniela.

ACT TWO

Later that evening, I wandered around the streets of Miracle Mile and downtown Coral Gables. I wound up in an area that consists of a square mile of cocktail bars, fine dining restaurants, museums, and boutiques. A homeless man arranging his cart drew my attention. The homeless man, better known as Orange, was tall and bearded, with kind eyes. He spoke with an Eastern European accent. His clothes were a few sizes too big.

"Hey, I'm on my way to the store—can I get you anything? Food, soda, beer, anything you like," I said. He looked at me, eyes wandering.

"Are you hungry?" I asked.

"Sure."

"How about some sandwiches, soda, and—"

"Okay," Orangc said.

"You like cola or lemon-lime soda?"

"Maybe... orange."

"Okay, I'll be right back."

"Okay, okay," he said.

I turned and walked in direction I came from. I lied when I said I was on my way to the market when I was on my way to the bar. Even the act of going there alone made me rethink my life choices whom I let in and what I want. I went from despair to brooding to optimism. If I can help someone else then I'm not at rock bottom then, but I'm still not calling Daniela. At the convenience store, I picked sandwiches, orange soda, water, and beer. I returned with my hands full of bags, which obstructed my view. "Here you go," I said, handing the bags to Orange.

"Thank you. Thank you," Orange said. I arrived at Mia's and sat on one corner of the modern rustic bar. A bartender, the historian type in his fifties, twirled a cocktail napkin in front of me.

"What can I get you?"

"Double whiskey on the rocks, please." The bartender served my drink, and I raised my glass.

"Cheers."

"Cheers," the bartender echoed, raising a glass of iced tea. Several whiskeys later, with my eyes barely open, I take another sip. This was the point where a responsible individual would ask for a cup of coffee. I put down my glass and stirred, my eyes slowly shut. The bartender must have noticed.

"Hey, hey, buddy." The sound of fingers snapping brought me around, and I opened my eyes.

"Welcome back," he said, placing a glass of water in front of me. I stood, looked at my bill, put money on the bar, and headed out. I wasn't broke, but I also couldn't afford any more slip-ups. This was the moment in the public service announcement when the friend who doesn't let friends drink and drive would take my keys, but I was flying solo. So, I pulled into a gas station for more booze. Money wasn't a problem for my inebriated self. I was on a *Viva Las Vegas* roll here, so I grabbed a six-pack out of the cooler, paid, and tromped out the door. And, well, beer is best enjoyed cold, so I did the next unconscionable thing and popped one open—I took a big gulp right there at the gas station. At that moment, I was just blocks away from my apartment, so I believed I was home-free. I placed the half-finished beer bottle in the cup holder, rolled up to the curb, and glanced at the cars approaching. I veered onto the road and pulled ahead of the approaching vehicles, my tires screeching. Suddenly, a police siren. *WOOP WOOP.* Red and blue police lights flickered off my rear-view mirror, so I pulled into a plaza. Then while submitting to a sobriety test, I toppled over, and the little optimism I had had been crushed, like my wrists inside those cold torture bracelets. Handcuffed in the back of the police car, I watched a tow truck hook up to my car. I tapped out, emotionally. A tear rolled down my cheek as I shamefully buried my head in my chest. My life was flashing before my eyes in red and blue.

"All right, the first case this morning is Josi Piriz. Mr. Piriz, you are charged with the following: DUI, alcohol or drugs, and driving with an expired driver's license. So, the total bond will be one thousand five hundred dollars. Broken down, one thousand dollars for the DUI and five hundred dollars for the expired driver's license. Is there anything else before me involving Mr. Piriz?" the judge said. And at that moment, my bar-bill hit me nearly as hard as my hangover. I was *Living La Vida Loca* in Miami where even celebs experience money woes and I was certainly no exception.

"No, your honor. But thank you very much for hearing us right away.

"And we appreciate your honor's courtesy," the public defender replied as I stood beside him with my head hung low.

And after hours of self-loathing, I finally got my phone call. The following day, outside the Dade-County Correctional Facility, Melchi's seated on a bench. So, I walked out of the building, saw Melchi, and gave him a slight smile. He grinned back at me. We headed toward the street where his car was parked.

"Oh, man—you going to need backup."

"Backup?" I said. Melchi raised his shirt, exposing his gun holster. With a smirk, I shook my head.

"I just have one question," he said.

"What's that?"

"You still a virgin?" I shook my head. Melchi laughed. We hopped in the car. After a short ride, we arrived at my condo. I raised my head and saw Daniela's baby blue Maserati with her *PRNCES* license plate. Boy, if there was anything that I tried to avoid, it was doing anything to prove that I was beneath her—and not that anyone had ever said anything to that effect, but her mother's eyes couldn't hide what she was thinking of me being with her daughter. All her family respects is status, a degree, or pedigree. They didn't respect income, since I leased princess's car.

"Good luck," Melchi said. I shot him a look and gave him a fist bump.

"I'll see you."

"Okay, man—see you on the news." I got out of the car and walked toward the apartment and threw a sideways peace sign in the air. Melchi gestured a cutthroat and rolled away, exposing his bumper sticker with the Punisher logo on his rear window and:

2ND AMENDMENT
AMERICA'S ORIGINAL
HOMELAND SECURITY

As expected, Daniela was too upset to go down to jail. But as I feared, she was sitting on a chair next to my bed.

"Hey," I said. Daniela stood, and I walked over to greet her with a kiss.

"Why don't you take a shower? You'll feel better," she said. I'd feel better once she'd told me what she was thinking. I nodded and walked into the bathroom and showered. I walked out of the bathroom in my boxers, and I threw on a T-shirt.

"Why did I have to hear what happened from Melchi?" Oh, boy. Time to think on my feet.

"You can't take calls at work." Daniela pointed to a bag on the nightstand.

"I got you a burger with extra sauce."

"Thanks." And after Daniela takes a breath she says,

"Okay, there's nothing we can't overcome, because we have always been a great team, and we've always been there for each other. And I have always believed that you have the potential and the swag to go places. And I want to be there with you every step of the way."

"And I want you there every step of the way," I said.

"Now, explain to me what happened."

"Durant," I said.

"Mm-hmm." Daniela's eyes were fixed on me while I connected my cell phone to my charger.

“Okay, I’m listening.” I touched her diamond-studded watch.

“I didn’t buy you this with tip money.” Daniela grabbed her watch.

“You stole it?”

“No.”

“Then what?”

“I never made any money in the stock market, because”—I paused—

“I’ve never owned a single share of stock.” *I thought I’d never have to admit to starting our relationship with a lie, but I really wanted to talk to her that night when I first saw her, but so did the rest of the guys at the bar. I almost felt as if I was competing for her attention, and I wasn’t sure being myself was going to sweep her off her feet. Who doesn’t want to make a great first impression? And then, I worried she’d think I was not only a loser, but a liar as well—though, it was time to come clean.* Daniela ran her hands through her hair.

“But you were yelling at someone, sell or buy, and you were cursing. I remember you slammed your drink down on the bar. It was the night we met.”

“I was just trying to impress you.”

“You didn’t have to impress me. Guys were hitting on me all night, and you were the only one I was interested in.”

“Well, you girls aren’t exactly a one-size-fits-all kind of deal. And you were the only girl in that bar I couldn’t take my eyes off.”

“Why did they fire you?”

"I provided certain amenities to the guests that the hotel frowns upon," I said, with my eyes scanning the ceiling as if the answers were up there.

"Like?"

"Like ... party favors and companions," I said.

"Companions?"

"Escorts."

"Escorts," Daniela echoed. She hit me and started to walk away.

"Real mature," I said.

"I'm not the one who threw it all away." Daniela stopped at the door.

Shame washed over me as I was once again confronted with my reality, I wasn't a wealthy stockbroker nor a medical Doctor—I was just a nerd, who escaped life by going to the cinema or burying his head in a good page-turner. I couldn't help the feeling of isolation from the world sometimes—it's as if I were meant to be alone, but who does? I want what most people do but does it all have to be so black and white? Daniela grabbed the doorknob and looked at me.

"My friends were right."

"About what, being sluts?" I placed my hand on Daniela's arm, and she yanked it away and cleared out with a slam of the door. Leaning back on the entrance, I slid down onto the floor. The next day, I watched Benjamin grab a beer out of my fridge, see his name on an envelope clamped to a magnet, and pull out a brochure. On the brochure: *LITTLE PALM ISLAND.* A folded paper fell out, and he retrieved it eagerly and unfolded it. The note read: *THIS TRIP WAS MEANT FOR YOU. ENJOY!* Lady Luck certainly knew how to put a smile on Benjamin's face. As I sneaked out, I imagined him dancing and spilling beer all over the floor. If I hadn't been hung up on Daniela, I would've enjoyed that trip with Benjamin, but, *c'est la vie.* I picked out roses at a flower shop. Roses that Daniela tossed into a dumpster outside of Saki's. Nothing says "tough chance" like a girl throwing away fresh, long-stemmed, red roses. Most women love receiving flowers and gloating. They don't just want to be loved, they want to be envied, especially by their coworkers. I figured it was too soon for her to give in and accept my apology for ruining her ideal future. This time, I tried a different, more subtle approach—I sent her a gift basket to her house. I was hoping that maybe she was playing it cool in front of her coworkers and that she was more likely to be softened when she was alone. I couldn't have been more wrong. Daniela grabbed a card out of the wine basket and tossed the card in the trash. Then she took the bottle of wine and walked out of her house, plunked herself down inside a white convertible Mercedes with the top down, kissed the man in shirt and tie who was sitting behind the wheel, and held up the wine bottle and laughed. The two reveled in my misery as they drove away. I stepped out from behind a bush with a bow-wrapped box in hand and walked down the street savoring a piece of candy. The sweetness of the indulgent truffle was no match for the bitterness in my eyes. As I threw the box in the trash, I wiped a smudge of chocolate from my lips. Then, a sigh of defeat, and I called Melchi. What's a guy to do when he's been dumped and humiliated? There's no better time for a little action.

"I'm down for whatever."

"Cool."

"Dale." When I got home, I set my phone down on the nightstand, looked at a framed picture of Daniela for a moment, then knocked it over. I lay in bed, absent, the TV watching me. Later, I was fast asleep, face down and across the bed, my feet dangling off the mattress, reading lamp and TV on. The soothing hum of the A/C muffled the sound of the TV. My cell rang. I answered.

"Yo ... All right." I put down my phone and laid out my faded blue jeans and sleek leather jacket. And as I washed up, my mind began flooding with thoughts of what was to com. The more I tried to avoid thinking about the mess I made, the faster the condemning thoughts came. Money problems, getting, legal troubles. But I already made plans with Mechi, so I gelled my hair, washed my hands, and felt my five o'clock shadow before heading out the door. As I locked up, Melchi rolled up to my building in his shiny white Range Rover Sport. I walked toward Melchi's car. He ended a call and looked in my direction.

"Look at you, man—you are ready for the Blue Oyster bar," Melchi said.

"Shut up," I said. I jumped in Melchi's car and greeted him with a handshake-into-half-hug.

"You ready to get crazy?" he asked, and I just looked down at the drinks sitting in the cup holders.

"Which one's mine?" I asked. Melchi handed me one. I took a swallow.

"Ahhh." Melchi reached into his shirt pocket and held up a baggy.

"We have to take it easy with this shit. This stuff—" Melchi shook his head. "will numb you face." When I reached into my pocket, Melchi handed me the blow. I took a hit with my key and choked a little.

"Good shit," I said. Moving my mouth and lips around, I handed back the baggy to Melchi.

"I told you." Melchi pushed off as I raised my cup and tapped with his.

"To micro-bikinis," Melchi toasted. We drove down the streets of Midtown, down a trendy, high-energy boulevard that was alive with stylish night owls dining and drinking in the mostly al fresco bars and restaurants. The brick-paved sidewalks and walkways were adorned by beautiful palm trees and sculptures. The buildings were covered in tasteful, colorful, imaginative street graffiti. The sidewalks mirrored an eighties fashion show runway, with endless models strutting their stuff. We arrived at the Spot, stepped out of the car, and headed for the entrance. A typical linebacker-type doorman with a ponytail opened the velvet rope for a redhead and a brunette.

"There's a fifteen-dollar cover tonight—live band." Melchi paid, and the doorman opened the rope.

"Enjoy, fellas." We walked into the Spot, a very funky retro lounge that looked like a cool museum-turned nightclub, glowing with soft pink and blue lighting, walls covered with pop art-inspired wallpaper, and an ambient, oversized onyx bar. Melchi spotted his reflection in the mirror and blew himself a kiss. A female bartender in ripped jean shorts and a tank top emblazoned with the word *Sexy* approached from behind the bar. Melchi extended his hand to the bartender, and she took it.

"We meet at last," he said. The bartender made a face but smiled.

"I'm Mr. Sexy," Melchi said. The bartender snickered.

"What can I get you fellas?"

"Double whiskey and more double whiskey," Melchi said, before hissing perversely and staring at the bartender's butt as she snatched the bottle of whiskey. Melchi's nostrils flared, and, with his tongue hanging out, he air humped.

"Let's do a couple shots. Only like two. Or ten, but that's it," Melchi said. The bartender handed us our drinks.

"Let me also get four tequilas, too." Melchi added. Suddenly, Melchi saw something. A man looked at me sharply, and Melchi walked around and stood behind him. Melchi's eyes fixed on him.

"Hey, you know my friend?" Melchi asked. The man shook his head.

Now, everyone knows it's impolite to stare at someone, even more so to mad-dog them, especially in the presence of their ride-or-die friend. But I don't need any more drama in my life, so I have to keep the peace.

"You have a problem with him?" Melchi continued. I grabbed Melchi and shoved him in the direction of the dance floor while the guy walked away.

"Fucking pussy," Melchi shouted. So, I pointed Melchi toward the dance floor, where he could blow off some steam.

"Wait up. My drink," Melchi remembered.

"I got you." I walked up double fisted while Melchi became absorbed in the crowd of girls on the dance floor. A shrug of the shoulder, and I coolly threw the drinks into one glass before heading for the men's room. After a trip to the urinal, I washed my hands. The attendant handed me a towel.

"Thank you."

Then I dropped money in the tip jar and grabbed a mint. Outside the men's room, I caught a glimpse of the redhead I'd seen at the entrance earlier. I contemplated my next move. The girl was Eli, easy on the eyes, shy, with an English accent, in her twenties. Eli was leaning back on the wall with her head down at her feet and one arm crossed across her abs. Suddenly, she raised her head in my direction and made eye contact, so I made my way over to her.

"Waiting for your boyfriend?" I asked.

"No. I don't have a boyfriend. I'm just waiting for a friend." Eli scanned the bar.

"She's talking to some guy." I studied her. She smiled sheepishly and looked down at her feet.

"I'm sorry. I just can't believe the most beautiful girl in here is standing alone in a corner." *Okay, so I dropped a cheesy line—but I was taken by surprise and spoke my mind—I truly believed she was beautiful on a level all her own.* Eli looked down at her feet and then into my eyes. And just before I could get in another word, she leaned in.

"You're ..." Eli gently planted a kiss on my lips.

"Eli," a girl called out. We turned our attention to a brunette as she drew closer. The brunette looked at Eli wild-eyed.

"Abi, this is—" I reached out my hand to Abi, who took it.

"Josi. Nice to meet you, Abi," I said.

"You, too ..." Abi gawked at me.

"Give me a minute," Eli told Abi, turning away.

"This place is so beautiful," Abi said to Eli.

The ride-or-die BFF is usually the second-best person a suitor can receive approval from besides her father. I'm not counting my chickens before they're hatched, but I like my odds. Eli pulled her purse off her shoulder, took out her wallet and keys, and handed them to me.

"Hold this, please." Then she dug in her purse for a moment and pulled out a business card and a pen. She wrote, "*Give us a ring*" on the business card and placed it in my hand.

"Okay," *I said.* Eli smiled and said,

"Call me." She reached in, closed her eyes, and gave me a lip-gloss kiss.

Her kiss lingered long after she departed, and my eyes were fixed on her till she was out of sight. Melchi walked out of the dance floor, checking out a girl.

"Ay yai yai," Melchi sounded off and grabbed his crotch.

"Two whiskeys," I ordered. I was celebrating with Melchi, but he had no idea we were celebrating the meet-cute that just took place. Melchi walked over to me. "Where did you go?"

"The bathroom," I said. The bartender served the drinks.

"You want to hit up Pink's?" Melchi asked. Pink's was a nudie bar. I chugged my drink and headed for the door. *Was it a night of debauchery just for the sake of it—just for blowing off steam—or was I trying to prove that I still had it with the girls? Or maybe I was hiding my insecurity.*

"Wait up, man," Melchi yelled as he followed me out. Two days later, I walked my bike inside my apartment and stepped into the bathroom. After a warm shower, I turned off the radio and walked sauntered into the kitchen, eyes fixed on the dirty dishes in the sink and all over the counter. Then I washed the dirty dishes, fixed myself a sandwich, and grabbed a carton of milk from the fridge. Inside my bedroom, I grabbed some business cards out of my nightstand and began flipping through them until I reached the one with Eli's number on the back. Then I took a bite out of my sandwich and a gulp of milk. *I thought to myself, "It's now or never, because soon it won't be rejection that I'll have to worry about—my insufficient funds will make certain of that".* I picked up my cell and dialed. The phone rang once, twice, thrice.

"Hello," she answered.

"Hi, this is Eli?" I asked.

"Hello, there, Eli," she joshed.

"I meant, is this Eli?"

"This is she."

"Hey, it's Josi. We met at the Spot."

"Josi?" Eli said.

"We met at the Spot two nights ago."

"Of course, I remember you, Irish boy."

"Um. No."

"I'm messing with you," she said.

"Cute. Very funny." Eli laughed.

"Would you like to catch a movie with me this weekend?" I asked.

"I have to check my class schedule."

"You have class Saturday night?"

"Saturday night ... yes, maybe we can catch a movie then."

"Awesome." There was some indiscernible chatter.

"I hope I'm not interrupting anything," I said.

"No, it's just us girls, you know ... girl stuff."

"Well, I have to get some work done, so I'll let you get back to your girl stuff."

"Okay. You'll call me Saturday?"

"Ah, sure, why not?"

"Oh, who's the funny one now?" Eli said.

"See ya later."

"See ya round." I clicked on my laptop and watched an eight-year-old boy breakdancing. On Saturday night, I drove up to Starbucks. Eli sat at an outdoor table wearing a charming white dress with little white embroidered flowers, so I made my way to her.

"You look nice," I said.

"Thank you," she said with a big smile. We greeted one another with a peck on the cheek.

"I checked the movie listings, and I didn't see anything special," I said. Eli pulled her phone out of her purse.

"That's okay, I'll just call Abi to pick me up. She must not be too far."

"What?"

"We were doing our nails together, so I had her drop me off." *WTF? Was there nothing else to do in the city?*

"Okay. So, not even a coffee?" Eli laughed, turned, and put her phone back in her purse.

"You had me going. Great poker face."

"You got it, dude," she said, making me laugh. I was relieved that she was only kidding because I was looking forward to getting to know Eli.

"Why don't you grab us a table while I get our coffees?" I said.

"Oh, okay."

"What's your poison?"

"Caramel Brulé." Eli took her wallet out of her purse, and I grabbed her hands to stop her.

"You must be kidding."

"Okayyy," she said. Moving ahead with my obvious ploy to hold Eli's hand, I admired her sapphire ring.

"It's my birthstone."

"I know." Eli winced.

"Stalking my Facebook?"

"Taking an interest in someone is hardly considered stalking." And after a well-earned smile, I made the line for coffee. Eli fiddled with her cell phone. I set the drinks down on the table.

"What are you having?" she asked.

"The same."

"Have you had it before?"

"It's one of my favorites as well," I said. We drank.

"So what—" I said, simultaneously with Eli, who said, "What do you—"

"You go—" I said, simultaneously with Eli, who now said "You—" Eli laughed.

"Yeah, maybe we should have those coaster type things from the all-you-can-eat steakhouse."

"Like Porcao?"

"Yes, exactly." Eli mimed that she was flipping over a coaster and nudged the imaginary coaster to me.

"You're up." I slid the imaginary coaster back.

"Ladies first."

"Fine, tell me something about yourself."

"What would you like to know?"

"If God gave you the power to change something to better the world, what would it be?" she asked.

"You're quite the anomaly—Tina Fey and Barbara Walters combined." Eli smiled and playfully hit me on my shoulder, cleverly copping a feel of my arm.

"I don't know, I guess I'd change myself, so that I can inspire others to do the same. I'd take risks. I'd write. I'd make movies, so I can spread love instead of hate, faith instead of fear. I know it's silly, but you asked for it."

"I don't think it's silly. Ambitious, but not silly," she said. Eli seemed to have an idea and stood, coffee drink in hand.

"Grab your coffee, I wanna show you something." I stood.

"Come on."

"Where are we going?"

"You'll see." Eli motioned for me to toss her the keys.

"My car's a stick."

"Just toss me the keys."

"Okay." I tossed her my keys, which she caught with one hand while drinking her coffee. We took a seat, with her in the driver's seat, placed our coffees in the cup holders, and buckled up.

"You have to—" I said, but was pushed back in my seat, the tires screeching, when she took off like a shot. I held tight on the "oh shit" handle, peeked through my hand, and then gave a sigh of relief. I got out of the deathtrap on wheels. Eli tossed me my keys, stifled her laughter, then minced her way across the hotel-like driveway and toward a palatial estate I'd noticed in the neighborhood before.

"This is your house?"

"Not quite, I haven't offed my mum and dad, yet." I looked at her wide-eyed. She was kidding I presumed, but thanks to *LMN* movies, those types of comments gave me pause.

"I'm just going to grab something," she said. I took another look at the sprawling house, sighed, then almost whispered to myself, "Ridiculous." *But as impressive as her family's house was, I could never be one of those guys who leaned on a rich girl for self-gain. Not that I was ascending to sainthood or anything like that, I was just confident that we were meant to exploit our own special gifts and stand on our own feet.* Eli returned toting a large brown paper bag, which I gallantly stored in the trunk for her, and then I opened the passenger door. *I'm a gentleman and I know a good thing when I see it. Which is what we tell ourselves when we like someone. But regardless, I'm always a gentleman.* We hopped in my car and rolled out of the drive.

"You know the park over by the library?" she asked.

"Yeah, sure."

"Let's go there."

"I know this great little French bistro."

"After this pit stop, we can go to that little French bistro. I *am* a little hungry. But I'll be frank with you—I'm actually a cheeseburger kind of girl."

"Really," I said, shooting her a look. She nodded. I smiled. We arrived at the park. The lights were on, and there was a soccer game in progress.

"I didn't bring my *Pumas*." Once we were out of the car, Eli tapped the trunk, I popped it open, and Eli led us toward a building across the park while I toted the bag for her.

"Come on." We scurried up the steps of a church with Greek columns, walked around back, and arrived at the door of a smaller separate building. We walked inside the church cafeteria, where we were greeted by an old man, who took Eli's brown paper bag. And as we took a seat near the entrance, he reached in the bag, handed out some sandwiches and placed the rest of them atop a long table filled with hot stations of food and drinks. The church volunteers served the homeless, standing in line to be fed. Eli waved goodbye to an old lady serving food, and the old lady waved back. Eli took me by the arm, leading me out of the cafeteria. A hand went up, waving amongst the homeless eating at a table on the far end. I saw Orange waving.

"Thank you for food and drink," Orange said. I acknowledged Orange, with a subtle hand gesture as I was trying not to attract attention or cause a distraction at Eli's church. Eli saw the interaction.

"You know Orange?" Eli asked, surprised.

"Kinda."

"He seems to have taken a shine to you."

"I'm pretty awesome. Or maybe he just likes your sandwiches." We laughed quietly. Eli shushed me. I stuck my tongue out at her.

"Maybe you can help me make them sometime."

"Maybe. So, what's Orange's story?"

"He lost his family in Kosovo where he was a liberation fighter."

Overcome with sympathy over Orange's loss, I shook my head and changed the subject.

"You sure you didn't have your butler make all those sandwiches?"

"Who said butlers make sandwiches?" Eli said.

"We can ask *Siri?*

Eli playfully hit me on my shoulder as we arrived at the car. I laughed it off. Eli smiled. Later, at a burger joint, we sat across from each other in a booth laughing. Eli grabbed a notebook in my hands, but she couldn't pull it away. We played tug of war with the notebook. Then I unhanded it, allowing Eli to look inside. A waitress cleared our table and served coffee, and I took a photo of Eli, who was turning a page in my notebook. EVEN LATER …

"Did you have an okay time with me?" I asked.

"It wasn't the worst date I've ever been on," Eli said.

"Wanna take another chance next weekend at the beach?"

"Okay. Who do you have in mind?" she asked.

"Uhhh, *Bradley Cooper*."

"Ooh, yes. He's much cuter."

"Well, call up *Margot Robbie,* and you've got yourself a double date." We laughed. On a sunny day at the beach, Eli and I raced to the water. I dove in as she tiptoed in and out, slack-jawed from the cold ocean. I walked over to grab Eli. But she saw me coming at her, so she started walking backward to get away from me. Eventually, I caught up to her and carried her further out. *SPLASH,* I tossed her in. Eli shuddered and stuck her tongue out at me, and I draped her in my arms. She gently pulled herself away, smiled, and casually submerged herself. We leaned in for a kiss, and I suspected something when suddenly she sprayed salt water into my eyes. She tried getting away but I dove in after her. She screamed as I picked her up in my arms and slowly pulled her in for a kiss. I never could've imagined that I'd have such a terrific beach day. Later at my condo, Eli showed me her portfolio of realistic paintings.

"Wow, these are paintings?" I asked.

"Uh huh."

"I find it hard to draw stick figures. You have a real gift."

"Well, I have been painting all my life."

"Modesty will not change the fact that you're a freak."

"Thank you, but there are a lot of amazing artists out there."

"And countless stars. But you are certainly special," I said as I held up a painting.

"Maybe I can use a cheerleader."

"Well come on, let's get some supplies at the art store." Eli shoved me and pulled me by my shirt for a kiss. Another day, I sat in my condo looking up DUI insurance quotes for SR22 on my laptop. Then I slammed my hand on the desk and grabbed my hair. And later, I filled out a job application online as my car got hooked to a tow truck and hauled away. Keeping up with the Joneses was a thing of the past. I rode the bus in a shirt and tie, holding a notebook filled with resumes that didn't embody me. I interviewed for a job sitting in front of a man in a suit. I interviewed for another job in front of a woman in a business suit. Later still, I walked into a temp agency where everyone was in business attire. This wasn't me, but I needed to make ends meet. Another evening, I slept on the bus in a suit and tie.

Another day, in my now nearly empty condo, I took cash from a woman as two men carried out my couch, leaving me with only a bed, TV, dresser, nightstand, and lamp. Melchi and I hauled boxes into a small efficiency with boxes scattered on the floor. I headed to an SUV, a Hindu driver at the wheel. Eli insisted on sending me an Uber.

"Eli," he called out.

"Yes."

"Making out good today?" I asked, after a moment on the road.

"Oh, yes. Many rides," he said into the rear-view mirror.

"Feeling, okay?"

"Yeah, my mind's just a little preoccupied. I'm meeting some people at my girlfriend's house."

"Meeting the future in-laws?"

"No, they're out of town. I'm meeting her friends. Her rich, cultured, Ivy League friends." The SUV pulled up to Eli's, where a collection of exotic cars filled the driveway.

"Take care," I said as I exited the vehicle.

"Mr. Eli," called the driver. I turned.

"Remember one thing. We all come from God," he said, with a hand to heaven. I nodded and thanked him. Then I made my way up the steps of the entrance. Once inside, a housekeeper led me to the veranda and pointed the way. I arrived at the gazebo, where a gathering of yuppies, artists, and yuppie artists was in full swing. Eli greeted me with her hands full. She planted a kiss on me and handed me a drink.

"How well you know me," I said. Eli studied me.

“You’re not you.”

“Are you gonna hand me a *Snickers*?”

“*Snickers? Oh, You’re silly.*”

“Maybe I just need to hydrate.” I took a swallow of my drink. Eli grabbed my hand and led me inside the gazebo.

“*Pardonnez-moi*,” she called out. A couple of heads turned to Eli, but the cacophony persisted, so Eli whistled like a pro, taking me by surprise and quieting the get-together.

“Thank you. I want to introduce you all to Josi.” And the spotlight was on me. Then the usual exchange of pleasantries between Eli’s friends and me. Later, at the patio bar, a few of us gathered around. I sipped my drink and quietly observed. Eli smiled at me from a distance while she entertained a couple. Abi noticed my silence and nudged Jasper, a thirty-year-old hedge fund manager, into interacting with me. Jasper had had a few, so he’s slurring a tad.

“Jasper,” Abi said, in an almost whisper.

“Okay. Okay,” Jasper responded.

“I’m sorry if we’ve been excluding you from our conversation, but I’m sure you wouldn’t understand”—Abi nudged Jasper again—“or be interested in finance or academia.”

“No, not especially,” I said.

“What do you do?” Jasper asked.

“Josi’s a talented writer,” Abi announced. I gave Abi a look. She squirmed, then mouthed, “Sorry.” *Abi’s a true BFF because she has no clue if I can even write my name.*

“That’s tremendous. What do you write?” Jasper continues.

"Well, I'm still working on my first project, and uh ... I'm not sure I can do it justice by putting it into words … yet."

"I thought writers were all about words?"

Abi struck Jasper subtly while Aidan, a fifty-year-old author, must've read my uneasiness. Jasper downed his drink and poured himself another.

"No, Jasper. Writers are all about emotion," Aidan said, then turned to me. "Don't you agree?"

"I couldn't agree with you more. Spewing meaningless words is the same as firing blanks; there's no impact"

"That's right. You're in good company with our dear friend, Aidan."

"You're ... what? In your twenties?" Jasper asked.

"Twenty-nine," I said.

"Aidan, how many books had you written by the time you were thirty?" Aidan pondered.

"Eight or nine." Abi's eyes closed as she shook her head and pulled a stumbling Jasper away.

"You're drunk," she yelled.

"But at least I'm not self-proclaimed." Aidan's wife, Zady, who was in her forties, approached me.

"Pay no mind to Jasper. He's about as spoiled as they come, and you happen to have the one thing money can't buy."

"A personality," I said.

"That, too. But I'm referring to Eli." Eli hugged me from behind.

"Hey," I said. Eli planted a kiss on me.

"What's going on?" she asked.

"We're going to The Spot," a girlfriend said.

"Yeah, we gotta go, too," another girlfriend echoed.

"Thanks for the booze," a guy friend of Eli's said on his way out. Hugs and kisses all around.

"Thank you for coming," Eli said and pointed.

"Drive safe. Buckle up." Eli turned to Aidan and Zady. Aidan made a face. "Nothing new. Jasper being his usual charming self," Aiden stated.

"I don't know what she sees in him," Eli said. Zady made a face. "Dollar signs."

"Let's do another spa day," Eli said to Zady, with a peck on each cheek.

"Anytime."

"It was very nice to meet you, Josi," Zady said.

"The pleasure's all mine."

"Thank you for having us," Aidan said to Eli. Aidan extended his hand to me. "Good meeting you, Josi."

"Likewise." Eli and I embraced. Later, inside Eli's house, Eli played a romantic piano piece as I stood by, spellbound by her grace. We locked eyes, brimming with affection. The music died. Eli smiled at me gently.

"What?"

"Is there anything you can't do?" Eli thought about it.

"Hmm ... no," she said. Then she pulled me down onto the duet bench and kissed me. Later, Melchi drove me to my mom's, where I sat on a love seat across from my mother, a frail woman with a cheerful disposition, flanked by her crotchety, paunchy, husband Julio. *Now, I do love my mother and keep in touch almost daily, but her husband makes my visits with her awkward. Not only does he not cut me any slack, but he may also affect my mother's notion of who I am.*

"You have to get your act together. Parties with all the drinking and all the people aren't going to lead to anything good," she said.

"Mom, I'm applying everywhere and to all the job agencies and all the dotcom recruiting agencies."

"Julio, with all the handymen you know, you can't find him work? Even if it's just temporary."

"Doing what?" he asked.

"Julio, anything," she said.

"You know how to lay tile?" I shook my head.

"You ever worked with a chipping hammer?" I shook my head again.

"A circular saw?" Another shake of my head.

"Carpentry?"

"No."

"You see, Teresa. He doesn't know how to do anything."

"What do you mean he can't do anything? He's always had good jobs."

"But all he knows how to do is office work and push luggage carts. And here in this country, you have to know how to do everything." Julio made for the door.

"Where are you going?" my mother asked.

"I'm going to get cigarettes." We watched him go.

"Give me just a minute," Mother said. She walked out of the living room. And after a moment, she returned and put cash in my hand.

"Mom, you're in no position to loan me money." My mother shook her head while pushing my hand away. She massaged her fingers.

"Your arthritis?"

"It comes and goes," she said.

"Don't worry. I'm going to pay you back."

"At least for now, we don't have to pay the mortgage. And when the time comes, we'll just have to find another place. God has never failed me."

"That's fine, *but* I'm still going to pay you back." I kissed my mother goodbye. "You want to pay me back? Honor the memory of your father. That's all I ask of you." I nodded and walked out. *Once inside Melchi's car, I felt sick with shame. As we drove away from my mother's house, I ruminated long and hard on what my mother had said—about the only thing she asked of me, which was going to be a tall order to fill. My father was a well-respected and beloved man in Cuba and Florida. He helped many families from our communist country who sought a better life in the States. Here I am taking money from my aging mother.*

"My mom shouldn't be helping me. It should be the other way around."

"One day you will." Melchi took the on-ramp to the highway.

Months later, on a beautiful sunny day, I decided to take a bicycle ride through the neighborhood of Coral Gables so I could take my mind off everything. The bright, colorful flowerbeds and trees and the palm trees lined the roads. What a soothing sight—with the refreshing, ambient breeze and the occasional chirping of a bird. That was until a black Mercedes backed out of a church and whacked me off my bike.

The driver swung open his door and a young woman jogging rushed to my side.

"You, okay?" she asked. I slowly stood while picking my bike off the pavement.

"I'm fine." The driver of the car, a gregarious priest in his fifties, six foot tall or so, spoke with a Polish accent.

"I am so sorry. Are you sure you're all right?" I walked my bike toward the church's sidewalk and adjusted my helmet.

"I'm fine." I adjusted my helmet.

"Can I give you a ride somewhere?" he asked. A sun shower began to fall.

"No, thank you. I appreciate it, though." The priest walked alongside me, reached into his pants, and handed me a business card.

"If you ever need anything." I tossed the business card in my backpack.

"Thank you, Father." The priest extended his hand to me, I took it. Then the priest waved out the window as he drove off. I waved back on one knee, tying my shoes. Weeks later, in court, a judge read the sentencing as I stood nodding at the podium. Community service and traffic school weren't on my bucket list, but they were certainly more appealing than a one-piece jumper. With trash-picker in hand, I picked up trash at a park. Thoughts of inadequacy consumed me. *I felt as if I was my own worst enemy. I am blessed with a considerate, talented, and inspiring girlfriend, and it makes it hard for me to believe that I deserve such luck. Not only do I find it difficult to imagine a scenario where I can do my father's memory justice, but to do right by this special girl.*

Another day, outside the entrance of my traffic school, I was greeted by Eli's warm embrace and smile. Later, I waited for my turn at the ATM line outside the bank. Once I reached the monitor and viewed my available balance of $-997.43, *I felt as if I was staring at a screen displaying my wealth. They say not to confuse your net worth with your self-worth, but there's a reason why it's cliché—it's the first thing one thinks of when stuck in a downward spiral. I believe it's especially true for men since social conformity and even the Bible prescribe that men are to protect, procreate, and provide. If I can't even provide for myself, how can I feel anything but inadequate? Even my couch surfer friend has a boutique now. Although he inherited it, I commend him for taking on the challenge of running a business he couldn't possibly understand in its entirety.* Then, at Benjamin's boutique, there was an impressive display of haute fashion, modern decor, and glamour models for sales associates. I was seated on an oversized chair. And after a long wait, Benjamin emerged from the back end. I stood and met him halfway. My eyes welled up.

"Hey, man. Do you have any work for me?" I asked. Benjamin grabbed my arm. "Walk with me," he said and led me out the front door.

"What's going on?"

"I'm just going through a tough time."

"I hate to see you this way." I just nodded.

"What work could I possibly have for you? You see my store. What could you possibly do for me here?" I just shrugged. After an awkward silence, I saw a sales lady waving for Benjamin's attention, so I patted Benjamin on the arm.

"Sorry to bother you."

"Benji," she called out. Benjamin looked at her, then at me walking away. Benjamin shook his head and went back to the store. One day of culminating misery later, there were empty beer bottles and coke residue all over my nightstand. Now I can add the shame of using my mother's cash loan to finance my apparent addiction. I was wearing the same clothes from the night before. Scruffy and rocking a pot belly, I struggled to sit up on my bed, reaching for an open, half-finished brewski on the nightstand, and chugged it. I walked over to the kitchen and pulled open the refrigerator door. Hunched over, I looked at an empty six-pack and closed the fridge. Then I opened the freezer. All I found was a box of waffles. I looked at the waffles, disinterested. As I closed the freezer, I spotted a bottle. I reached into the back, pulled out a bottle of vodka, and looked at it, baffled. I removed the top, took a swig, and cringed. I took a prescription bottle out of the top drawer of my nightstand and popped some pills. I leaned back on the headboard, drank vodka from the bottle, flipped through channels, and tossed the TV remote. My cell phone rang. I looked at my phone sitting on the nightstand, brooding. I put the bottle on the nightstand and picked up the phone, eyes brimming with tears.

"Hello," Eli said. I wailed.

"Josi, what's wrong?" I broke down and cried.

"What happened?" I was unable to answer. Maybe it was because I was out of answers, and I couldn't get a word out—emotions had the best of me. Darkness consumed all of me.

"Talk to me. What's wrong?" I wobbled as I reached for the pill bottle and grabbed it off the nightstand.

"I just wanna go in peace." I had uttered words I never imagined could come from my mouth. *How'd I get there? Where was my head? I was overwhelmed with thoughts of inadequacy, failure, and fear. But talking about our feelings is discouraged among us "real men." We're taught to be macho, unshakable, even stoic—if one shows signs of weakness or fear, you're labeled a sissy or a coward—what man wants to be thought of as a pussy. We were brought up watching Clint, Norris, and Bronson.*

"Have you gone mad?"

Tears rolled down my face as I cocked my head and poured the bottle of pills into my mouth. It was nothing more than an attempt to relieve the rotten feeling of shame.

"Don't be stupid," she shouted. At that moment, I washed the pills down with the vodka, and my phone fell to the floor, breaking apart. I kneeled and picked up the cover, spotted the phone under the nightstand, and stood. Then, I staggered, tripped on a towel, and *WHACK*! I smacked my head on the edge of the nightstand, rendering me unconscious. I was laid out on my back. Blood dripped down my forehead and onto the white tiled floor. The door of my efficiency swung open as a piece of door frame broke away. Two police officers rushed inside, followed by two paramedics. At the hospital, Eli touched my hand as I lay sedated. She kissed my forehead. Later, near the entrance, I lay upright on a gurney in a gown. Paramedics stood nearby, heeding instructions from an administrator. A woman and a little girl sat in the waiting room near me. The shorty faced me and smiled. I smirked, then looked at the paramedics. She waved her tiny hand. I turned back to her as she briskly hid her face in the lady's arm. I smiled. Another look from the shorty, and she hid again. The woman said something to her. The paramedics rolled me toward the exit. The little girl sang, "Don't you worry, don't you worry, child. See, Heaven's got a plan for you." At a mental health facility, flowers, plants, and pastel colors spruced up the simple yet charming lobby. I was assigned a comfortable bedroom with a roommate who was never there, so I had plenty of time to reflect. *How am I going to be able to afford this, most might ask, but I'm just grateful to be alive. And the medication I'm on helps me not think too much. Maybe I needed some time to unpack the emotional baggage that's been wearing me down.* And upon arrival, "Don't you worry, don't you worry child. See, Heaven's got a plan for you," was stuck in my head. Was a song that I'd heard many times on the radio now a message for me? Was this a message from my dad? Was he trying to tell me that it was going to be all right? *Lately, I've been thinking more about my dad. People have been reminding me of him. Not that I need reminding because I don't, but it's nice to keep his memory alive. He was filled with so much life and had so much love to give. It feels as if he's truly watching over me, maybe even guiding me.*

"You have a visitor," a staff member said, interrupting my thoughts. I walked out to the lobby, a little shamefaced. Eli and I traded smiles. She gave me a tender kiss just beneath my eye as I rested my heavy heart in her warm embrace. Eli took it all in.

"You have to take care of you." Eli dropped her gaze. I did, too. She put her hand in mine.

"I brought you some things," Eli said. She motioned to the sitting area, and we sat. She opened the duffle bag, sifted through it, and took out stuff.

"I packed your mouthwash, toothbrush, toothpaste, shorts, t-shirts." Seeing Eli look after me that way put everything in perspective. I'd been so focused on living up to social constructs that I hadn't realized how lucky I was that Eli didn't conform to the materialistic world or its inhabitants. *Or else she wouldn't still be hanging around a guy like me, with problems like these. She just wanted someone to break bread with and talk to. But I judged her because of her status, so I never let her in.*

"I got your favorite cheeseburger"—Eli was almost in tears—"but they didn't have the sauce you like."

"Oh, come on, now. I'll be all right. I'll manage without the sauce." Eli laughed as her cell phone rang.

"This is no time to joke," she said. She went into her purse and pulled out her phone.

"Hello. Tell Marcia to get the file from Silvia ... Yes, it's already finished. I'll be there shortly." Eli put away her cell phone.

"I'm sorry. I gotta get back to the office." I stood and draped over her. A tight squeeze from Eli. She took a moment.

"How's the food?"

"Surprisingly good," I said.

"When can you go home?" Eli asked.

"The doctor said a couple more days."

"Okay, I have to get going." Eli grabbed her purse.

"You'll call me to come get you?"

"Worry not, fair maiden. This spiffy establishment has arranged a transport." Eli shook her head and stifled a smile.

"Oh. I nearly forgot." Eli reached into her purse and handed me a book titled *I Can I Must*. Eli kissed my forehead and scurried off. The receptionist buzzed me back in. Days later, I got out of the transport vehicle and walked around the house to my efficiency. As I stepped inside, I ran my hand over the repaired door frame. I looked around at the mess, picked up clothes, grabbed a garbage bag, and threw out empty beer bottles, soda cans, fast food bags, and pizza boxes. I cleaned and organized it. After a time, I lit a scented candle, threw myself on the couch, admired my freshly cleaned room, reached into my duffle bag on the floor next to me, and pulled out the book Eli had given me. I read for a bit. Then there was a knock at the door.

"Who's there?" I said.

"It's Benji." He wore a linen suit, an extravagant watch, and an absurd pair of sunglasses.

"What's going on?" he asked.

"Nothing special," I said.

Benjamin removed his shades.

"Come in. It's been—"

"What happened to your forehead?" he asked.

"I fell. Playing soccer in a rocky field." I pointed to the bandage on my forehead.

"It wasn't such a good idea."

"I called you, but I got your voicemail."

"Yeah, I was out of town. I forgot to pack my charger." Benjamin observed my tiny efficiency.

"Where did you go?"

"Oh, just to visit some friends in Naples."

"Italy?"

"Florida."

"Have you found a job?"

"Yes, I'm working with Melchi."

"Oh, yeah? Doing what?"

"We find fixer-uppers with potential. We buy them, renovate them, and put them back on the market."

"You're flipping houses."

"And other things."

"And how's that going?"

"It looks promising."

"What happened to your apartment?"

"I had to downsize to have more cash flow to invest." *I was quick on my feet tongue.*

"And where's your car?"

"I told you, man. I'm downsizing. It's about keeping your head above water during these difficult times." *What an asshole. He saw I was uncomfortable with this line of questioning, but he persisted.*

"Josi, save the bullshit for someone else." I looked up at the ceiling, feeling frustrated. What the heck happened to encouragement, support, and compassion? Then I let out a breathy laugh. I was busted.

"What do you want me to say? Maybe God's been trying to tell me something."

"Yeah, he's trying to tell you to get your shit together." I nodded.

"I am. I'm gonna write a movie."

"*Pfft, h*a, a movie? What are you going to do, move to L.A?"

"And whatever else it takes."

"Really?" Benjamin picked up the book Eli gave me and shot me a look.

"What's wrong with it?"

Benjamin looked at his cell phone and stood.

"This guy's made a fortune by selling false promises." By then, Benjamin was agitated, and his hands joined the conversation.

"Do you know how many piles of scripts by experienced writers who went to the best of the best film schools never even get read?"

"I know."

"What makes you think yours will be any different? What connections do you have?" Benjamin went on. I shook my head, shrugged, and followed Benjamin to the door.

"Come on, Josi. You have to get these pipe dreams out of your head." *All I could think of was holy shit. I wasn't expecting a life-altering motivational speech, but this bullshit was discouraging.* Benjamin grabbed the back of my neck.

"I'm just looking out for you. You're better than this."

"I know."

"What you need now is stability. You know, a nine-to-five with benefits. I gotta get back to the store." Benjamin leaned in close, almost secretively.

"I just got a Bertram 31." Genuinely happy for Benjamin, I put my arm around his shoulder.

"That's awesome, man." I walked Benjamin out. He pulled out of the driveway in his big, black, shiny new Mercedes and rolled down his window.

"I just finished renovating my house. When I have a barbecue, I'll call you."

"I'll bring my appetite."

Then, with one hand on the wheel and the other with a stogie to his chops, Benjamin peeled out. Then, inside the efficiency, my cell phone rang. I rushed back in. Hello. *Is this Josi Piriz?* Yes. *This is Sal from Bella Pasta.* Oh, how are you, sir? *I'm short-staffed. Are you still interested in the dishwasher position?* Yes, I'm very interested, I said pacing the room. *Are you available to start Monday morning?* Definitely. *Okay, we'll see you on Monday morning at eight o'clock.* Okay, thank you. Goodbye. *I'd been brooding over a job for a much-needed income, and the timing of such good news couldn't have come at a better time, especially after the world's most uninspiring speech.* The next morning, my cell phone played jazz. With my head stuck to the pillow, I felt around my bed and silenced my phone alarm. I rolled to the edge of my bed and slid onto my feet. I knelt and bowed for prayer. I was meeting Eli's folks that night. It's not that I lacked sophistication—I charmed the pants off my five-star hotel clientele—it's that I knew that she was the one for me, and you know what they say, "You only get one chance to make a good first impression." So, after an honest day's work at Bella Pasta, the Italian restaurant where I finally got a job as a dishwasher, I tossed out the trash and took off my apron. Who was I kidding? I did feel a little uneasy about the awkwardness of an intimate dinner with Eli's parents, especially after seeing their colossal residence—but I couldn't be stressing over a pile of bricks—it was their approval that I wanted. Ruminating about the evening ahead, I washed and primped as if I were attending the Oscars. Looking in the bathroom mirror, I arranged the collar of my polo under my sports coat, opened the medicine cabinet, and took out a pill bottle. Breathing a little heavily, I popped a pill and washed it down with a handful of water from the sink. *I wasn't worried about killing myself with pills, I know what landed me in the hospital was an accident, and if I hadn't been drinking so much, I wouldn't have been talking foolishness. Why was I breathing heavily? I asked myself. What was the reason for my sudden anxiety? Was the physical and verbal abuse I experienced as a child the catalyst of my unwarranted insecurity? And those stupid and scary panic attacks. I feared the future outcome of my decisions. But why? I was a good man. A God-loving man. I believed in the goodness in others. What was I always so afraid of? I guess I felt the need to prove myself to everyone.* So, I had dinner with Eli and her parents. Mr. Matias was a Cuban American entrepreneur, and Mrs. Matias, an enchanting Englishwoman. We dined at La Palme d'Or, an upscale restaurant in the historic Biltmore Hotel. The backdrop was mystical, with Old World charm. Sixteenth-century chandeliers lit the beautiful fresco murals in muted colors adorning the ceiling. Eli grabbed her napkin and wiped the ketchup off my mouth. I shot Eli a self-conscious grin as I picked up my glass of water.

"Josi's an aspiring writer," Eli said. I choked on my drink, and Eli patted me hard on my back.

"Eli is very optimistic and encouraging, but the truth is ..." I cleared my throat. "Excuse me. Um, I haven't written anything yet. It's more of a hobby, for now."

"Well, did you know, Josi, that Walt Disney spent hours playing with miniature figurines?" asked Mrs. Matias.

"No, ma'am. I wasn't aware."

"His hobby of collecting miniatures is said to have led to the creation of Disneyland, or at the very least influenced—"

"Yeah, yeah, yeah. And bippity-boppity-boo. Work your"—Mr. Matias looked around, making sure no one else was listening—"ass off." Surround yourself with the right people. Always be diplomatic, but don't take shit from anyone." Mrs. Matias shot her husband a wince of disapproval.

"Iggy."

"I pay my taxes." Mr. Matias raised his champagne flute, Eli raised hers, then I. Mrs. Matias shook her head at Mr. Matias, then finally raised her glass and clink-clanked with Eli and me.

"Will you be having any dessert or coffee this evening?" our waiter asked. Mr. Matias looked around the table.

"Babe?" Eli called me.

"No, thank you. I'm good."

"Just the check, please, Manny." Then, after a moment, Mr. Matias signed the bill and handed it to the waiter.

"Thank you, Manny. You're always such a great host."

"Thank you, Mr. Matias. Have a safe journey." Mr. Matias stood and took Mrs. Matias's mink off her chair and assisted her as she put it back on. Later, at the hotel entrance, he said,

"Josi, it was wonderful to finally meet you." Mrs. Matias kissed me goodbye. "Keep your head up," she said. Eli gave her dad a hug.

"I instructed Joaquin to take you wherever you want to go," Mr. Matias addressed Eli and me.

"He's on the way."

"Okay," Eli said.

"Have a pleasant journey," I said. Mr. Matias shook my hand.

"And thank you for dinner, sir." A look from Mr. Matias.

"Ignacio. And my pleasure, Josi." And with a tighter grip on my hand, he said, "You take care of my little girl."

"Always." A moment later, Eli and I stood outside the entrance of the hotel, waving at her parents as they were driven away in a black limo. Eli blew a loud whistle with her fingers.

"I have a surprise," she said. I loved surprises, even more so, when the occasion was no occasion at all. But I played it cool. *And maybe to Eli, this was a special occasion, since her parents and I finally met.*

"You're my surprise," I said. Then the headlights of a black town car washed across us. Normally, I would've asked for clues about the surprise, but I was just grateful that dinner hadn't turned into an interrogation. So, we hit the highway. Eli's head rested on my shoulder. I looked out the window as the reflection of the moon danced with the ocean. The town car drove over a bridge. A sign on the side of the road read *BIG PINE KEY*. Boat marinas, seafood restaurants, and tiki bars lined the streets. Beautiful tall pine trees and deer everywhere. I guess Eli recalled me saying in passing that I loved the Florida Keys. The town car pulled up to a multilevel house with a pool. It was a clear, breezy night. The stars sparkled in the sky, the water glistened under the moonlight, a bird chirped, and then another. A deer crossed the road. Joaquin, the muscular head driver, opened the car door for Eli as I stepped out the other side.

"Thank you," Eli said to Joaquin.

"My pleasure, Ms. Eli." I gazed at the house in subtle astonishment and followed Eli inside. We walked inside the tiki chic house.

"Holy Kokomo," I said. Eli switched on the A/C.

"What?" Sweat ran down my forehead. So, I complained in an English accent, "I'm sweatin' me bag, madame."

"I just switched on the air." Eli returned from the sleeping quarters, and I nestled her in my arms.

"What do you think?" she asked.

"Isn't this where Jimmy lost his ... shaker of salt?" Eli punched me softly, I feigned an injury, and then she pulled herself away, walked to a spiral staircase, and turned to me.

"I placed fresh towels in the bathroom for you, and there're plenty of my dad's Tommy Bahama outfits in the master bedroom. I'll shower upstairs." Eli climbed the spiral staircase, and I raided her father's wardrobe. Later, we walked hand in hand toward the tiki bar, which had all the bells and whistles of a traditional tiki bar. A live band played The Beach Boys. And the timing of Eli's surprise couldn't have been better. A much-needed weekend of distraction from the humdrum of my life. Eli was the only good thing in my life. She was the antidote, yet my understanding that a man needed to stand on his own began to have an insidious effect on me. We drank and danced the night away. I stirred my whiskey, and Eli sipped her pi□a colada through a funny-looking straw. It was a full house that evening. Eli and I had bedroom eyes for each other and danced face-to-face. When we returned to the Keys' house, Eli and I dodged raindrops as we made our way upstairs. Eli seduced me with every sensual sway of her hips as she walked over to the couch, grabbed a remote, and played music. Our eyes locked with smoldering passion. The music hit a crescendo as we stepped toward each other. I took my shirt off. Eli let the remote slip from her hand. She undid her dress, and it slipped to the floor, leaving her in boy shorts and a bra. I dropped my shorts and kicked them away, exposing my Calvins. Eli straddled me and I put her up against a wall. We both got a hand on my boxers and pulled them halfway down my thighs. Rain pounded on the windows; palm trees swayed outside. We got lost in a kiss as raindrops splashed on blue pool water. Eli grabbed my crotch.

"Wait. Wait," I interrupted and pulled up my Calvins. Call me crazy, but maybe there was a sound reason for abstinence till marriage. I was struck by this sudden epiphany.

"What's wrong?" Eli asked.

I sat on the couch while she turned down the music. Eli sat by me. I leaned over, resting my face on my hands, taken aback. I wanted Eli badly, but my instinct ruined the moment. I turned to Eli.

"I want to go all the way with you, but I feel this is not it. Maybe if we wait and deepen our relationship, it can be something truly special—you make me believe in love as a real-life fairy tale."

"I thought it was the whiskey."

"Okay," Eli said, placing her hand on my leg.

"I may need a magazine." We looked at each other, held our laughter, then couldn't keep it back anymore. At the break of dawn, we lay in t-shirts and shorts, partially covered by a blanket on the living room couch.

"And your dad?" Eli asked. I sighed.

"A pile of rebar fell on him and killed him" Eli shakes her head.

"I'm so sorry," she said caressing the palm of my hand.

"He was a construction welder—good with his hands. He could do anything. But what I admired most about him was his love for life, his generosity, and his curiosity. There were always two or three books at a time on his nightstand. And you could say that same curiosity in him stirred up my own. And it led me to ask him if he ever had a dream. And he said to me, that, in Cuba, he only dreamed of being free. And, after I was born, he just wanted to get me out of the country, so that I could chase the dreams he never stood a chance to." Eli took this with a warm smile and a nod, then caressed my face. I turned my head to get a better look at a wall photo.

"Hey, who's that guy in the photo with your dad?"

"That was my brother, Fin. He overdosed on drugs." I caressed her arm.

"I'm so sorry."

"He was talented. He sang and played several instruments. He was the lead singer of a band. They even had a record deal." Eli's eyes welled up

"But no amount of recognition could ever satisfy him. He was never happy with himself. And yet, he always made everyone smile." Eli rested her head on my chest.

"You know something?" Eli looked up at me.

"I think your artwork is going to grace the walls of some well-known art gallery one day."

"You're biased."

"And you're a badass and you know it," I said.

She smiled a little.

"I mean that—I believe in you"

"So much that I want to learn French." Eli gave me a look.

"I'm serious. I want to learn about art. And I wouldn't be against learning French, so we can visit the Louvre, and I can share your appreciation for all the things you love about art. And oui, madame, wiz a touch of sophistication."

Eli kissed me. And later, our town car drove over a bridge and passed a sign. *MIAMI*. At my efficiency, I sat back on my bed and after reminiscing about the amazing time I spent with Eli this weekend, I began reading the book she had bought me. Suddenly, there was a loud banging on the door, so I rushed to open it and Eli bolted inside.

"What's going on?" I asked. She dropped her purse on my bed, placed her hand on her waist, and sulked.

"What happened?" I reached for Eli's arm, and she pulled away before I could grasp it. Eli caught sight of a prescription bottle on my nightstand, walked over to pick it up, examined it, and put it back down. Then she found an empty bottle of vodka behind the bed and turned to me.

"You're killing yourself." *I went to detox after an accidental overdose, but my faith and confidence were renewed by the overwhelming compassion, love, and support from Eli. She never judged me or tried to change me, and that's why she took me to the Keys, world-famous for its salt life, offering plenty of relaxation and, well, a little intoxication. Just when everything seems to be coming together, it somehow comes crashing down. I'm plagued by trials and tribulations. Why, God, why?*

"The pills are for my anxiety."—Then I pointed to the empty vodka bottle— "And who knows how long that's been there?"

Eli headed for the door. I rushed past her and blocked the exit.

"Wait a minute," I said. Eli forced her way out, almost knocking me down, and headed impulsively toward her car as I followed her.

"Eli, wait. Let's talk." Eli held down the button to unlock her car and reached for the door when I grabbed her arm.

"I can explain."

"Can you explain the drugs and the prostitutes?" With bated breath, I tried to find the right words to say but wound-up blank.

"I didn't think so." And she slammed the car door on me. I pulled on the locked handle.

"Eli, please, that's in the past. I swear." Eli backed out, and I walked frantically toward her car. I watched her speed off, my arms flailing helplessly. Then I paced inside the efficiency, walked through the neighborhood, and went inside a gas station convenience store. I put down a six-pack on the counter. The amount on the register was $10.15. So, I picked up the beer, shamefaced and walked to the back of the store and put it back. I looked inside another cooler, grabbed a four-pack of cheap beer, and paid. I walked out with a bag of cold ones in hand. Across the parking lot, I saw my ex-girlfriend Daniela sitting in the passenger seat of her friend's car. She looked in the mirror, scrutinized her make-up, and applied more. Her friend, a slutty brunette, wore a short, skintight dress and heavy makeup. Waiting for her tank to fill, she tapped Daniela on the shoulder.

"Hey, isn't that your ex?" I pretended not to see them. And her other friend, a slutty blonde with her breasts pouring out of her child-size top, leaned forward to get a better look at me.

"Oh, my God. He looks homeless," said the brunette.

"What happened to him?" the blonde asked.

"Loser," Daniela muttered.

Later, I rode my bike to Benjamin's house, which was big and beautiful. It had luxury cars in the driveway, including a yellow Ferrari parked on the lawn. *I know for a fact that the Ferrari isn't Benji's because he didn't inherit Bloomingdale's.* So, I walked my bike across the lawn, set it by a bush, and walked around to the patio where Benjamin was barbecuing. Two friends of Benjamin's, Tommy and Shawn, sat in patio chairs, drinking.

"Hey, where have you been hiding?" Tommy asked and stood to give me a handshake-into-half-hug.

"It's good to see you, brother."

"Likewise." I walked over to Shawn, who was seated, and shook his hand.

"What have you been up to?"

"Not much," I said.

"You still working at the hotel?" Shawn asked.

"No, I'm between jobs."

"What happened?"

"Irreconcilable differences with management."

"I'm sorry to hear that."

"Eh, God's got bigger plans."

"Wait, weren't you writing a movie?" Shawn gave Tommy a look, who shook his head and stifled a laugh.

I tapped Benjamin on his shoulder while he flipped over meat at the barbecue.

"What are you doing here?" Benjamin asked.

"It's nice to see you, too."

Benjamin followed me inside the house. I helped myself to a scotch while one of the two girls chatting turned her attention to me.

"Hello," I said. Then I waved and skedaddled with my drink. Benjamin tailed me out to the patio.

“Hey, man, I’m sorry to do this to you, but we’re going to have dinner now.”

“Hey, man, it’s cool. I’m meeting some friends on the mile.” Then I chugged my drink as I approached Tommy, who gave me another handshake-into-half-hug.

“Take care of yourself, brother,” he said.

“All right, you too.” I waved at Shawn, who was still seated as I walked toward the gate, grabbed my bike, and slipped out.

“Ay, Josi, hold up.” Staggering across the driveway with my bike, I stopped as Benji approached.

“What’s up?” I asked.

“Next time, call before coming by.”

“Are you serious?”

“Yeah, man, you can’t come to my house drunk.” I stared at Benjamin.

“You kidding me right now?”

“Josi, I’m serious. You come here drunk, unannounced. We have dinner guests, and you’re drinking the only bottle of scotch we have to offer them. You just help yourself without asking.”

“I had one lousy drink.”

“I have a girlfriend now, Josi. She doesn’t like drunks.”

“And you’re the poster child for AA now?”

“I’m sorry man.”

At my efficiency, I walked my bike inside and shut the door. Then I sat on my bed watching a movie while enjoying a sandwich when a program reminder popped up on the TV.

I reached for the remote on my nightstand and accidentally kicked a beer can over, spilling beer on my bed.

"Oh, shit. Shit! Fuck!" I lunged toward the spilled beer can to salvage what I could of my troubled soul's antidote. Then I grabbed a towel, wiped down my bed, and while inspecting the beer-soaked area, I saw the image of a frowning Jesus left behind. As I stared at the perfect image through my tears, I wondered if I'd lost my way. I lay in bed. The lights were off, TV was on. Then a proverb was superimposed on the TV. *ISAIAH 55:9 AS THE HEAVENS ARE HIGHER THAN THE EARTH, SO ARE MY WAYS HIGHER THAN YOUR WAYS.*

I was riveted by the words coming out of this pastor's televised sermon. It felt as if he was talking exclusively to me. The proverb he was addressing was speaking right to my heart. Either the alcohol was making me hallucinate, or this pastor was channeling God's divine intervention. I'd grown tired of suffering and living in fear of failure. I was burdened with feelings of inadequacy, shame, and hopelessness. I had nothing, which meant that I had nothing to lose.

The next morning, lying in bed, I reached for my phone. 5:30 a.m. After I walked out of the bathroom in a t-shirt and shorts, with my hair still wet, I headed out on my bike, pedaling fast. After I arrived at Starbucks, I locked up my bike, walked inside, and made the line. As night fell, I was still at Starbucks. Crumbled paper and pens lay around me as I wrote in a notebook. Back at my place, Melchi helped me carry a headboard to a young couple's pickup truck. Another day, I wrote on my bed, which was just a mattress. Later, a man helped me carry a gray recliner from across the street toward my efficiency. I jogged in the street and signed for a delivery, and the UPS guy handed me the package. Then I typed on my new, used recliner. I ripped sheets out of my notebook, crumpled them, and tossed them to the floor. After a snooze on my cozy recliner, with my hands still on the keyboard, I awakened from a peaceful sleep, rested and ready to follow my heart and turn my *battles into blessings. These three words from the pastor's sermon the other night struck a chord in my heart.* I slid a flash drive into the USB port of my laptop to save a story I was anointed to write—*and not just any story, but a message from God channeled through my God-given talent. It felt like it was time to turn this talent into my God-given gift to be shared with the world. The time had come to answer my call.* Upon arriving at the UPS store, I locked up my bike and walked inside, where I used a three-hole puncher to bind my script. After paying the man at the counter, I walked out under the sun-kissed sky, closed my eyes, and felt peace come over me. Back at the efficiency, I sat on my bed and typed in the Google search bar: *How to sell a screenplay.* And later, I sat on my bed, nodding off with the laptop open. On the laptop: *WE DO NOT ACCEPT ANY UNSOLICITED MATERIAL.*

Then again, on another day: *SILVER SCREEN STUDIOS. WE DO NOT ACCEPT ANY UNSOLICITED MATERIAL.*

And again, on another day: *SCREEN GEM STUDIOS. WE DO NOT ACCEPT ANY UNSOLICITED MATERIAL.*

Again still, on another day: *FIRST TAKE STUDIOS. WE DO NOT ACCEPT ANY UNSOLICITED MATERIAL.* I stared at the screen, rolled my eyes, then got up and walked away. Later: *WE DO NOT ACCEPT ANY UNSOLICITED MATERIAL.* I sat up and typed. Then: *SCREEN WRITING AGENTS DO NOT HAVE TIME TO READ YOUR SCRIPT.* Defeated, I closed my laptop, leaned back on my pillow chair, and shut my eyes. Slouched on my pillow chair, hands resting on the closed laptop, I was fast asleep. Then I set my laptop aside, flipped through a book of business cards, and pulled one out. I clutched my cell phone and dialed while pacing around the room.

"Mick … Oh, I'm sorry … Okay, okay. Call you in twenty ... Thanks."

I sat at the edge of my bed tying my sneakers while making another call. Rode my bike. After arriving at Bella Pasta and made yet another call, which went straight to voicemail. And then another and,

"Hey, Mick, Josi from the Sumay Hotel … Yes, I understand, I have a lot going on myself—" The door swung open, and Sully, the owner of Bella Pasta restaurant, a no-nonsense husky Italian man, walked outside carrying a box.

"Josi," he hollered, so I covered the mouthpiece on the phone and looked up at Sully.

"I need you to take out the trash. One of the coolers broke last night, and it stinks in there."

"Right away, Sully." Sully threw the box in the trash and went back inside.

"—They just called me into a meeting, so I'll cut to the chase. I finally wrote that script I pitched you at The Sumay and you had mentioned something about an agent, a friend of yours ... I won't embarrass you ... I promise you; I've done my homework. And I wouldn't be asking if I didn't think it was ready ... okay ... I sent it to the email on your business card … bye" *The Sumay wasn't just for the rich and famous—it was a springboard for all those who dared to dream, connections galore!* In the Bella Pasta restaurant bathroom at dusk, my phone rang as I was untying my apron.

"Hey, Mick ... I owe you big time ... right, no second chances with Hollywood ... down to the bones ... okay, see ya soon." I got a high five from a coworker who helped me put on a jacket. I ran my fingers through my hair and took one last look in the mirror. I arrived at the Starbucks inside a talent agency building and took a seat at a table inside. Mick approached accompanied by Stan, a tall man, with dyed jet-black hair and eyebrows. And I stood to greet them.

"Hi, Josi," Mick said. We shook hands.

"Thanks for taking the time. I—"

"Just be yourself," he said in a low voice.

"This is Stan."

"Pleased to meet you, sir."

"Josi, in *Hollywood,* we're all friends—call me Stan.

"I'm going to grab something inside. Can I get you anything?" Mick asked Stan.

"I'm fine. Thanks." Mick points to me.

"Josi?" I reached for my wallet, but Mick motioned that he was paying.

"I'll have a tea, thanks."

"You know which kind you want?"

"Chamomile."

"It's too loud in here at this hour. Why don't we go up to my office," Stan said.

"Sure," I said. *A million thoughts running through my mind—mostly of the wicked kind.* Mick returned with our drinks and handed me a mammoth cup of hot tea. Stan got up. I followed him.

"We'll be back," Stan announced.

"Okay," Mick said. So, I grabbed my tea off the table and followed Stan into his small high-toned office. Stan cued me to take a seat.

"Take a load off," he said as he walked over to a liquor cabinet while I sat.

"Would you care for a drink?"

"I'm okay, thank you. Stan poured himself a drink, placed his glass down on his desk, and picked up my script.

"I read your screenplay. And I'm not going to lie to you." He paused.

"It needs work. But it's got potential." Stan polished off his drink.

"Josi, tell me. Can you see yourself directing this movie?"

"I mean, I'm a fast learner. I'm an absolute sponge."

"Can you act?"

"I was the male lead in a high school play."

"Is something wrong with your tea?"

"No, it's just scolding hot."

"You should take the lid off and let it cool off."

"Thank you."

"What if I told you I could make you a star?"

"Where do I sign?" Stan pointed across the room toward a doorway.

"Go in there and look at the photos. Take your time. Ponder the notion of one day having your photo on that wall." I walked through the door, and after a moment I returned from the other room, impressed.

"You see what I can do for you?" I nodded.

"Wow."

"Are you willing to let me guide you?"

"Absolutely." I sipped my tea.

"You'll do anything?" Stan asked.

"Anything," I said. Stan sat next to me as I was holding up my cup to take a sip when suddenly Stan forced my free hand to his unzipped groin. *I felt foolish, angry, and deeply disappointed. Although I wasn't versed in the art of breaking into the movie business, I wasn't naive about the inevitable obstacles that come with any significant endeavor.* Without hesitation, I emptied my cup of scalding hot tea on his bare crotch.

"Ahhh," Stan yelled, dropped to the floor in agonizing pain. I grabbed my screenplay from Stan's desk.

"You bitch," he yelled. I barged out of the office, leaving Stan on the floor. I scampered toward Bella Pasta as the sky began to turn gray. I felt my eyes narrow and had to force them open. *I sensed I'd been drugged—a tell-tale sign of the ambitious role God has chosen me for in the battle between good and evil. And I'm emboldened knowing that "Fortune favors the bold."* Then, at Bella Pasta, I stood in the doorway of the back office, running my fingers up and down the edge of an envelope while Sully was sitting inside writing at his desk. Sully stood as I took off my apron and turned it in. *I've been let go.* Melvin, a waiter with dorky glasses, a Pee Wee Herman hairdo, and a squeaky voice, approached.

"Ay, what's up, Josi?"

"Hey."

"Are we all set for dinner?" Sully asked Melvin.

"Just about," Melvin said.

"You going out tonight?" Melvin asked me. I shook my head. Then Sully must've noticed I was avoiding eye contact with Melvin, who was unaware of the situation. Frustrated by Melvin's intrusiveness, Sully got face-to-face with him.

"Go see where you gotta go."

"Oh, my bad." Melvin walked away.

"If it picks up again, I'll call you," Sully said. I nodded and made for the back door. Sully shook his head and nodded toward me as the manager in a shirt and tie approached.

"I hate losing this kid, but what I'm gonna do," says Sully to the manager. Later, birds flitted about and squabbled over breadcrumbs as I sat on a park bench, plucking breadcrumbs from my half-eaten sub. Later, I placed a dollar in the offering box, lit a candle, and knelt in prayer. Another day, at my efficiency, one man rolled in a hand truck as the other handed me money. They carried away the few pieces of furniture I had left. Afterward, the men waved from a cargo truck, and I shut the light off in my emptied efficiency. Well, what used to be my efficiency. Then, at Melchi's place, I put down my duffle bag in a corner of the living room while Melchi rolled in my suitcase and tossed his keys onto the dining table.

"Help yourself to anything in the fridge," Melchi said. I sat on the couch.

"Don't worry. I'm gonna repay you."

"You don't have to pay me nothing, man. Come on. You would give your shirt off your back to anyone," he said.

"And look what it's done for me." Melchi placed a blanket and pillow on his couch.

"Are you kidding me, man? You know how many guys would give anything to has what you got?" Unable to bear the situation, I shut my eyes. *Not that I was finished, but one might say it was a "Dark Night of the Soul."* "Yeah, man, close your eyes, because you so blind anyway. Come on Josi, you can do anything. You can write. You can talk. You are so persistent; you are freaking annoying. But what you think?" Melchi signaled toward the door.

"Espielberg going to come knocking at your door?" Melchi sat beside me and handed me a box of tissues. I looked at the box of tissues and then at Melchi.

"*You got two choices in life. You can cry for what you lost*. Oh, my pussy hurts. *Or you can fight for what you want*." I knew Melchi was intelligent, but I had no idea there was a motivational speaker inside him.

"Did you Google that?"

"It's good advice." Melchi tapped me on my leg and slipped away as I mulled over his words.

"Hey, how do you know I can write?"

"I read your journal."

"You read my journal?" I shook my head as Melchi slipped away.

"It sounds good. Big words." I walked toward Melchi's bedroom and stopped short of it.

"Hey, you know I can help you with your houses. I paint like shit, but I can pressure clean, cut grass, throw out trash."

"You bet you ass you gonna help me." I cracked a smile and walked back to the living room. Then I knelt by the couch with my head bowing for prayer.

"Goodnight," Melchi hollered.

"Goodnight," I said.

"Don't be jacking off all day, man." After a subtle smile and a head shake, I resumed praying. Then the next morning, I yawned my way toward the kitchen, turned my attention to the dining room table, walked over to it, and picked up a note: ***"I belief in you asshole"*** I laughed, walked toward the kitchen, poured myself a shot of Cuban coffee, and nuked it. I sat at the dining room table filling out an entry form for a screenplay contest on my laptop. I attended a film conference with a guest panel including Stephen Baldwin, the American actor, director, producer, and author. I was seated two rows opposite him. The audience applauded. The conference host approached the podium.

"That's all the time we have. Thank you all for coming. Please drive home safe and have a good night." With my backpack in tow, I made my way down the amphitheater, weaving my way through the crowd, and exited. I managed to reach Stephen Baldwin and his entourage as they walked toward another room. Flashes from paparazzi cameras illuminated the dimly lit conference area. A lady pulled the door shut as I arrived and made eye contact through the windowed door, which she opened enough to stick her head out. I raised my lanyard ID.

"I'm a screenwriter. I just wanted—"

"I'm sorry, he's in an interview," the woman said.

"Media only."

"I understand." As I peered through the windowed door, the woman opened it forcibly, nearly knocking me over.

"I'm sorry. You can't stand there. You have to wait upstairs, like everyone else," she said.

"I was just—" And after being cut off, the conference lady locked me out. So I jostled through the fans in another attempt to intercept Stephen Baldwin. *I was trying to do what any crazed, passionate, and amateur scriptwriter would do, which is to thrust his script in a producer's face at the most inappropriate moment.* And this time I hit a dead end in the form of a conference room divider. As Stephen Baldwin headed out, his entourage surrounded him. The onlookers were at his heels. In one last-ditch effort, I dashed for the rear exit. Stephen Baldwin approached a black SUV while the paparazzi snapped shots of him waving to the crowd. I emerged as the SUV pushed off. I sighed, flailed, and kicked a piece of paper on the ground as I distanced myself from the mayhem. I took a seat on a bus bench under the gray sky. After a moment, I reacted to raindrops. My eyes were fixed on a charming Spanish Baroque-style church with an appealing lined palm tree walkway, so I took the walkway. The drizzle intensified, but I paid no attention to it.

I took the steps to the entrance, found the front door closed, plodded down the steps, and headed around the side in search of another way in. Suddenly, the drizzle turned to rain, forcing me to run back up the steps. Rain poured down as I sat and waited it out under the arch of the entrance. I took off my lanyard, tossed it in my backpack, and, rummaging through it, pulled out my cell with a business card stuck to it. I squinted, trying to make out what was on the card, and used the flashlight on my phone to see. On the business card, I read, *FT. ALEKSANDER KEDZIERSKY C.E.O. ELYSIAN FAITH FILMS USA.* Rain poured heavier. I held the business card to my heart and looked to the heavens, threw the card in the backpack, and made a call. With a cheered-up smile and phone up to my ear, I sat against the door, talking. Some days later, I ended a call and received an email from FT. Aleksander Kedziersky, CEO of Elysian Faith Films U.S.A. I began reading what he'd written: *COVERAGE*

OF SCRIPT. I scrutinized every word of it, scrolled down some pages of a report, put my head down, and pounded my fist on the table. *My initial reaction was, of course, disappointment. However, after ruminating for a while, I realized that without coverage from industry experts, I would be lost in oblivion. I came to the realization that writing is rewriting.* Later that night at Melchi's place, I typed away on my laptop as Melchi and a girl walked out of Melchi's bedroom in nightclub attire, red cups in hand. Melchi messed with me by trying to close my laptop, forcing me to grab it. The girl ran her fingers through my hair before following Melchi out the door. I waved without ever taking my eyes off the screen. A few days later, indiscernible chatter spilled into a reception area where Melchi sat tapping the keys on his phone and looking up at the hot receptionist talking on the phone. She hung up.

"You sure you don't want anything to drink?" the hot receptionist asked.

"No, thank you." As she dropped her head, Melchi eyeballed her while biting his lip. Then I walked out of the office.

"A-yo, wait up," Melchi hollered as he followed me out.

"Talk to me, man." Melchi was now flanked by a woman hugging files and me, all facing the elevator. Not a peep or eye contact between Melchi and me on the elevator ride down. *He was dying to know what happened, and I was still taking it all in. But apparently, Melchi was apprehensive about asking me what just happened, since he'd seen what the aftermath of the disappointments looked like.* Melchi approached me on the sidewalk, placed his hand on my shoulder, and looked up at me while my eyes welled up. We paused. Then an awkward silence was interrupted by my laughter. Melchi read me.

"Oh, man. You such an asshole," he said. And then he punched me on the shoulder. I laughed, and Melchi gave me a bear hug before bouncing me up and down. We locked arms and bounced around and around, elated. I was beside myself, experiencing an almost out-of-body experience. My dad had to smile down at me. And I didn't have to sell my soul to the devil. All I had to do was believe.

ACT THREE

Months later, on a movie studio lot, I shook hands with a man wearing sunglasses and a ball cap. There's no greater feeling than that of fulfillment, especially when it serves a greater purpose than us. And now I get to answer the oftentimes condescending question,

"So, what do you do?" And with a smile, I say, "I make movies—you know, the Hollywood kind." Six months later, Daniela stood outside Mia's restaurant with her two girlfriends, waiting for a table as I walked past them, pretending not to see them. I was clean-cut, shaven, and greeted by a man in a suit. Mia's was thick with people, so the suit parted the crowd for me with the assistance of a uniformed police officer. Daniela's girlfriends looked at one another, wide-eyed.

"He cleans up nicely," the slutty blonde commented. The slutty brunette stepped on the slutty blonde's foot.

"Ouch, what?" The slutty brunette cringed at the slutty blonde. Daniela rolled her eyes. Benjamin sat alone at the bar. I walked toward the bathroom when suddenly I felt someone tap me on my shoulder. I turned, facing a bleary-eyed, disheveled Benjamin, with a drink in hand.

"What's up," I said. He smiled sheepishly.

"Hey, man." I gave Benjamin a handshake-into-half-hug. Benjamin shifted in his seat, with eyelids drooped.

"I'm sorry," he said.

"For what? Please." Benjamin pursed his lips and gave me a love tap on the shoulder.

"I've been wanting to talk to you."

"Everything good?" I asked. Benjamin burst into cynical laughter and motioned to the bartender for another drink.

"Oh, Josi." He slid his hands down his scruffy face.

"What? Your girlfriend?" Benjamin took a drink, shook his head, and unraveled.

"I lost my stores."

"What?"

"Tommy fucked me."

"He sold my stores right from under me and ran off with all my money."

Benjamin swirled his drink.

"And Gabriela? I asked. Benjamin replied by dropping his gaze. *The once smug Benjamin had been humbled into inescapable humility, and I reflected—gloated inside a little. Another might have delivered the coup d grace, but I stayed on high ground.* Benjamin threw back his drink, slid the glass forward, picked up another drink, and huddled over it.

"Gold-digging whore," he said. Benjamin took a swallow of his drink.

"Hey, don't beat yourself up. Anyone can fall for a scam." Benjamin's expression was tragic.

"What you need now is stability." I patted him on the shoulder, and as we faced our reflections in the mirror, I continued,

"You know, a nine-to-five, with benefits." And I walked away, leaving Benjamin staring at himself, his reflection as vacant as his circumstances. Later at my mother's, mom sat at her sewing machine, struggling to open an envelope with her letter opener. She squirmed and moved her hand around in agony. She adjusted her reading glasses and found a signed, blank check enclosed. Written on it was, *FOR MORTGAGE—PAID IN FULL*. She stared intently, her eyes glistened, and she let out a sigh of relief as the burden that had lifted was suddenly replaced by a profound sense of gratitude and disbelief. She thought I was in the bathroom, but I was standing quietly outside her doorway witnessing the most gratifying moment of my life before sneaking off. And in another part of town, Orange stepped out of a taxi, and I walked him toward a two-story building where he turned the key to a beautiful, fully furnished apartment. Orange set down his army green duffle bag, walked over to the refrigerator, grabbed an envelope taped to it, and pulled out a note. On the note: *Welcome home, Orange.* And he opened the fridge to find it well stocked with a door full of orange soda. Orange nodded to the heavens and smiled at me with welled-up eyes. I read somewhere that success is not measured in the number of dollars you make but in the number of lives, you impact. I truly believed that. I also believe that people should treat themselves. So, I treated myself to a magnificent three-story smart home with an elevator, elegant design, marble and wood floors, double stairs, and a pool. Not too shabby. I stood in front of a dressing mirror in my bedroom and buttoned up my black dress shirt. I was clean-shaven, and fit, with a classic hairstyle. I wore a sharp black exquisitely tailored suit with a sapphire-colored silk handkerchief, the same color as Eli's birthstone. Facing the mirror, I threw my jacket on, remembering my eight-year-old self, a boy, combing his hair in front of the mirror when this woman yelled at him in her Cuban accent, "You think you're some kind of movie star?" I saw the boy bury his head in his chest. Head buried in my chest now, I arranged my collar. Then I raised my head and straightened the lie of my tie in the mirror. I took a breath and headed out the bedroom door. I walked down the stairs of my house. *I liked the sound of that. "My house"*. I got in my car, a classic white Ford Bronco, and pulled out of my driveway. Then I pulled out of a drive-thru with some Chipotle for this homeless man who always greets me with a warm smile. And later, I got in my car and set down an assorted flower arrangement on the passenger seat. Later still, I came to a rolling stop, handed a bag to a homeless man holding a sign on a street corner, then drove away. The homeless man unwrapped the burrito and smiled to the heavens. Then I drove over a bridge. The skyline reflected beautiful pastel colors shimmering off the ocean. I arrived at Perez Art Museum Miami. Light wood floors, grand crystal chandeliers, and floor-to-ceiling windows overlooking the bay made up this architectural marvel. With flowers in hand, I wandered around trying to find Eli. After a time, my eyes found hers. I watched her from a distance. She sparkled in her glittering dress. I beamed. Then out of nowhere, a handsome man with puffy, golden-blond hair approached Eli. With red roses in hand, the handsome man dipped Eli and gave her a big kiss on the lips. He carried her and spun her around. I walked inside the bathroom, tossed the flowers in the garbage, opened the faucet, splashed water on my face, and wiped my face with a paper towel. Then after looking in the mirror, I looked inside the garbage and found the flowers undamaged in a clean, empty garbage bag, so I picked up the flowers, took a deep breath, and out I went and straight toward Eli. The handsome man held Eli's hands while talking into her ear. Eli laughed. Then she seemed to freeze. Her gaze was fixed on me as we locked eyes. I walked toward her. We met. For a moment, there was an awkward silence. The handsome man's glance flicked over to me, then back to Eli.

"Aren't you going to introduce us?" the handsome man said.

"Yes, of course. This is—"

"Josi," I said.

The handsome man extended his hand to me. I took it.

"Victor."

There was a moment of awkward silence.

"I'm going to get a drink at the bar," Victor said. He caressed her arm.

"Some champagne?"

"No, thank you." Victor nodded to me.

"Would you like a drink?"

"No, thank you."

"I have to meet up with my girlfriend," I said.

"Well, the night is young. You must come back with your girlfriend."

"We'll see." Victor stepped away, and I handed Eli the flowers, kissed her tenderly on the forehead, and walked off. As I was going, a whimper escaped Eli. I slowed up, wondering—stopped. Watching her turned away, with her face buried in her hands.

"Hey. What's the matter?" I handed her my handkerchief, and she wiped her tears.

"You came here to tell me you have a girlfriend?"

"What's the difference—you have a boyfriend."

"Who says?"

"Says the kissing and dancing you and your Prince Charming had going on."

"Please. Victor's gay."

"Bullshit."

"No. He is. See for yourself," she said, pointing. I turned and saw Victor coquettishly straightening another man's tie.

"I'm happy for you," Eli said, pointing out my polished appearance. She took a moment to collect herself.

"You got all you ever wanted." I closed in.

"Almost." Then I kissed her. And after a moment, Eli pulled away.

"Wait, don't you have a girlfriend?"

"You gave up on me," I said. Eli dropped her gaze.

"You broke up with me. Remember?"

"I went to see you, but you moved and changed your number. You just disappeared." I considered her words. And she was right. I had vanished. *There was no doubt in mind, that she was telling the truth—why wouldn't I—she believed in me before I did.*

"You still haven't told me if you have a girlfriend."

"You tell me." Eli's face relaxed, and I leaned in. Eli leaned in. Our lips locked, and we got lost in a kiss. After we came to, a painting caught my eye. It was a painting of a young man at a desk. And when I took a closer look, I saw the man with a pen in his mouth, stargazing, and a blank page before him under a shooting star. It was a painting of me at a desk. And our lips meet again. Months later, on my way out of Melchi's apartment:

"Wait, you animal," Melchi hollered.

"What? I gotta go," I said, fiddling with my keys by the door.

"Look at me, asshole." I looked up and saw Melchi holding out a gift-wrapped box.

"What's this for?"

"Yeah, you know, man, since you such an asshole, and you no gonna be here for you birthday." I shook my head.

"I open it now?"

"No, man. When you do your taxes." I unwrapped my present and pulled out an Oscar replica trophy, with *"ASSHOLE AWARD TO JOSI PIRIZ BEST ORIGINAL FRIEND "BELIEVE" ALWAYS,"* engraved on it.

"This is—"

"You like it?"

"I do. But you've done too much already."

"Aha, sure. You think I forget all you did for me? When we was in high school, I had no money, no friends, and you always buy me lunch." I hugged and kissed Melchi's face–he pulled away with a swift elbow shrug.

"I always know you a homo."

"You know you like it," I said. We half-assed hug-into-handshake. Then he nudged me into the hall and slammed the door shut behind me. I departed, admiring my shiny new flask. The following evening, fresh-cut flowers, a framed wedding picture of Eli and me in Paris, and vibrant paintings added a softer touch to my sophisticated yet stolid dwelling. In the kitchen, the phone rang and rang and rang. Wrapped in a towel, Eli picked up a cell phone off the kitchen counter.

"Hello. Hold on, let me check." Eli surveyed the living room and looked at the oven clock. 9:18. She looked toward the front door and saw a keyless car key on the wall table. Eli picked up the phone.

"He's probably walking the dog." Eli walked down a hallway and out of sight. Later, the front door opened, and I arrived with our very excited toy golden doodle named Sunny. Once unleashed, Sunny charged toward Eli. Eli petted him. I did a double take on Eli, sensing something was wrong.

"Is something the matter?" Eli gestured for me to sit next to her on the couch, so I sat, and she caressed my arm. She said nothing. *I sensed something wrong, and turned to stone, my eyes fixed on Eli.*

"What?"

"Melchi's gone." I looked up at the dimly lit ceiling.

"He lost control of his car and hit a light pole."

"No! Not Melchi!" I shouted. My eyes fixed on the ceiling.

"Not Melchi! Why, God, why?" Eli grabbed my hand as I collapsed onto the couch in tears. Then at the mausoleum for Melchi's burial, a priest swung a thurible around Melchi's coffin as friends and family were gathered. Eli stood by my side. *I wondered about Melchi's final moments—whether he knew they were just that. Was he scared? Were the angels there to take him home? I questioned if I could've done something to prevent his death. The what ifs spun around my mind like a revolving door. My best friend had been taken from me, and it was way too soon.* One year later at the Dolby Theater, Eli and I sat in the audience arm in arm, and a male presenter, flanked by a beautiful woman, announced the winner.

"And the Oscar goes to..." *I closed my eyes, took a deep breath, and thought to myself, "No matter the outcome, I have already won. I have no regrets."*

ACKNOWLEDGMENTS

Every story begins somewhere—and mine begins with gratitude.

First and always, to **my Lord and Savior, Jesus Christ**. You are the Light behind every step, the Voice that whispered, *keep going.* Without Your grace, this dream would have remained a quiet wish. Through You, I learned that faith doesn't wait for miracles—faith creates them.

To **Mary Kole**, whose insight and editing brilliance helped me discover the rhythm within my words—thank you for helping this vision find its true form. To **Alexander von Ness**, whose artistry gave my dream its face, and **Slim**, whose design brought its soul to life—you both turned imagination into something real.

To my **mother**, who began as a skeptic and became my greatest believer—thank you for showing me that love can transform doubt into faith. To **Nikki**, whose early encouragement helped give this story its first heartbeat, and to **Dennis**, thank you for sharing her light with my dream.

To **Sol** and **Ivonne**, my constant cheerleaders—your belief was the echo that kept me going. To **aunt Nena**, thank you for the small comforts that quieted my restless mind. And to my

brother, for your steady presence and endless support—thank you for always being there, in every way that mattered.

To **Paul** and **Alex Ruiz**, thank you for giving me the chance to work, to grow, and to fund this vision—because dreams require faith, but also fuel. To **Eric**, for building something from nothing beside me, proving that great things can rise from humble beginnings.

To **Mari**, who introduced me to the power of vision boards—thank you for showing me that when you can *see it*, you can *be it*. To **Mayda**, your generosity and kindness provided the space where this dream could unfold.

And **Raul**, my deepest gratitude. From the moment you handed me *The Script* by Alyn Darnay, you planted a seed that changed everything. You believed before I did, and that belief became my compass.

To my circle of brothers—**Jota**, **Roy**, **Cesar**, **Tony**, **Alex G**, **Jay**, and **Chino**—thank you for the laughter, loyalty, and light. To **Nick**, for arranging the path that led to stability and renewal. And **Angel**—keep being Angel, so I can keep soaring.

Each of you is a scene in the story of this dream. Each of you played a part in turning belief into reality.

This book is living proof that when faith leads and vision follows, the impossible becomes inevitable.

And for that, with every beat of my heart—**I thank you.**

Believe, and it will be.

ABOUT THE AUTHOR

I am a writer driven by the belief that words have the power to heal, challenge, and quietly transform the human heart. Long before I ever considered the mechanics of publishing, storytelling was already shaping how I made sense of the world. Writing, for me, is both craft and calling—an act of meaning-making rooted in empathy, truth, and lived experience. Through my work, I aspire to inspire, entertain, and gently impart wisdom. We all need a good laugh, a deep cry, and the occasional nudge that helps us see ourselves more clearly. If my words can offer any of that, then they have done their job.

My path to writing has not been a straight line. I have worn many hats throughout my life, living and working in Florida, Indianapolis, and most recently Los Angeles. Each place added another layer to my understanding of people—their contradictions, longings, and quiet resilience. These environments became classrooms, teaching me how to observe closely, listen carefully, and recognize story not only in dramatic moments, but in the small, often overlooked details of everyday life.

One chapter of my journey placed me behind the scenes of a world far removed from solitude and quiet reflection.

I worked for an international superstar on a world tour, witnessing firsthand the intensity, pressure, and spectacle of life at the highest level of public attention. While exhilarating, the experience also sharpened my awareness of the difference between noise and meaning. It reinforced my desire to write work that prioritizes substance over spectacle—stories that linger not because they are loud, but because they are honest.

The deeper foundation of my writing, however, was formed much earlier. I survived a troubled childhood that required resilience before I had language for it. Like many, I carried those early wounds into adulthood, where they eventually manifested as addiction. Recovery became one of the most pivotal chapters of my life. It demanded honesty, accountability, and compassion, and in return it offered clarity and self-awareness. These experiences continue to inform my voice on the page, allowing me to write with empathy rather than judgment, and truth rather than pretense.

I also endured four long years in a deeply unhappy marriage—an experience that challenged my sense of identity and tested my emotional endurance. While painful, it became an unexpected teacher. It stripped away illusion and forced me to confront what I truly valued: integrity, freedom, and authenticity. The lessons learned during that time were hard-earned, but they were not wasted. They now live on as emotional truth within my writing, enriching my characters, themes, and narratives with depth that cannot be manufactured.

Everything I write is shaped by the understanding that life is rarely simple, and growth is rarely linear. My stories often explore redemption, perseverance, faith, humor in dark places, and the courage required to begin again. I do not write from theory or distance; I write from experience. My characters are informed by people I have known, versions of myself I have outgrown, and questions I continue to wrestle with. I believe readers can feel the difference between emotion that is imagined and emotion that has been lived.

Now, at the age of 49, I find myself living a life once confined to imagination. It is not defined by perfection, but by purpose—and that distinction matters deeply to me. I approach writing at this stage of life with gratitude rather than urgency, aware that every chapter behind me has sharpened my voice, and every chapter ahead offers an opportunity to use it with intention.

Writing remains my chosen medium because of its intimacy. A book asks a reader to slow down, to enter another mind, and to sit with ideas long enough for them to take root. That quiet exchange between writer and reader feels sacred to me. It is where vulnerability meets trust, and where transformation becomes possible.

Armed with a lifetime of experience—my personal artsenal—I believe the pen is still mightier than the sword. Words can soften what the world has hardened, illuminate what has been hidden, and remind us of who we are capable of becoming. If my writing leaves the reader feeling seen, encouraged, or less alone, then I have fulfilled my purpose.

This work, and this journey, are only the beginning.

www.ingramcontent.com/pod-product-compliance
Lightning Source LLC
LaVergne TN
LVHW011029110826
845149LV00015B/3341

9798994689004